PRAISE FOR ISLAND CHAINS

"I had the pleasure of working with Patti through the Institute for Public Safety in the Florida Keys. Her stories of the Keys reflect her experience with criminal justice professionals and this brings strong realities to her book. We often spoke of what brings people to the Keys and the answers were always the same. The beauty of the islands is obviously the main draw. The laid back atmosphere (island time) is also a lifestyle many dream about, and well if you love the sea and all it has to offer, then there is no place better to call home.

When we reflected on the role criminal justice professionals would face working in the Keys, a darker side would emerge. More often than not, my conclusion was that if you were not born and raised in the Keys, you ended up there because you were running from something. Whether it was a broken marriage or relationship, maybe a crime and for some, just the cold weather from up North, many people show up without a plan and can be quickly drawn into making bad decisions. This was the backdrop for this book and I found it accurate portrayed some of crimes we were aware of.

Drugs, human trafficking, robbery and violence are all realities in our communities. This book reflects those realities and serves notice that even in paradise you may not be immune to the experience. I hope you enjoy *Island Chains* as much as I did."

-MARC HALVORSON, RETIRED DIRECTOR, INSTITUTE FOR PUBLIC SAFETY,
FLORIDA KEYS & RETIRED LAW ENFORCEMENT OFFICER

"This novel shows that even 'paradise' has a darker side. Explores the underbelly of island life. It's an awesome look at the other side."

-INVESTIGATOR CHRISTOPHER MATTSON, FLORIDA
FISH AND WILDLIFE COMMISSION (FWC)

ISLAND CHAINS

PATTI LAVELL

OTHER BOOKS BY PATTI LAVELL

*Confessions of a
Catholic School Dropout*

Fat Chance

ISLAND CHAINS

PATTI LAVELL

ROCHESTER, NY

Front cover design by Rachael Gootnick.
Back cover and book design by Nina Alvarez

For permission to reprint portions of this book, or to order a review
copy, contact: editor@cosmographiabooks.com

ISBN-13: 978-1-7322690-5-7

CONTENTS

To the survivors.

Of hurricanes, violence, addiction, and neglect. May your light shine in spite of that or those who try to dim it.

"Every form of addiction is bad, no matter whether the narcotic be alcohol, morphine or idealism."
-Carl Gustav Jung

"Even paradise could become a prison if one had enough time to take notice of the walls."
-Morgan Rhodes, *Falling Kingdoms*

DAY ONE

STELLA

Everybody does it, that's what Stella told herself.

Then donning a mask made brittle by the sun, she prepared to slip off the back of her fifteen-foot fishing boat.

She'd forgotten her gloves, which was unfortunate. Her prey was called a spiny lobster for a reason: its sharp spines could go right through just about anything. In past trips, even with gloves, she'd return home with more than one wound from a temperamental little bugger, and today was no better. Her hands were scraped and pierced, and she suspected a piece of antennae had even broken off into her right palm, but she'd have to deal with it when she got home.

But that would be later. Stella didn't want to head back without a pile of lobsters. God knows she failed at something damn near every day, but today had to be different. Her husband had finally made a life-changing promise to her, and it warranted a pot full of delicious seafood. If only Louis could hold up his end of the bargain.

"Whatcha doin', neighbor?"

Stella jolted. She'd had been so lost in thought, she hadn't heard the twenty-two-foot Bayliner sneaking up on her. In fact, it was so close to her little craft that she had to stick out her foot to keep the vessels from banging together.

"Enjoying the water. You?"

"Oh, just doing my job. Making sure no one's pulling lobster before Mini Season starts."

Stella busied herself with the uncooperative strap on her mask. She knew the penalties would be stiff if she got caught, but she didn't frighten easily. She fought bigger demons than Dave Grody on a daily basis.

"I'd hate to see a neighbor go to jail for out-of-season fishing, but the Sheriff's Office trusts me to be their eyes and ears, ya know. Not much happens 'round here I don't know about. Arrested Steve and Julie Peterson last week for taking lobsters out of the canal. Damn shame, but they had it coming."

"Sure. They had it coming."

Dave Grody volunteered with a group of retirees who, as far as Stella could tell, got hard-ons doing free safety inspections and making life miserable for people like Steve and Julie Peterson, not to mention Stella herself. The previous winter, Steve had been let go from the nuclear power plant in Homestead when his Parkinson's kicked into high gear and he could no longer hold a pen. Julie waited tables at the same diner Stella did, but without Steve's income, they could barely buy groceries and pay the mortgage. They relied on Mother Ocean to provide much of what they ate. As far as Stella was concerned, arresting those two for catching their dinner was like arresting a homeless person for picking from a mango tree on a vacant lot. But sure, they had it coming.

Grody puffed out his chest. "We all have choices in life. Bad choices lead to bad things, ya get me, Stella?"

Stella side-eyed Dave. He looked like a bad Guy

Harvey ad. Pressed, woven shirt covered in sailfish tucked into a pair of pleated, navy blue cargo shorts. She was pretty sure he used hairspray—his wavy mop never moved no matter how fast he ran his boat, or his mouth.

Oblivious to Stella's mental inventory of his attire, he put one waxed leg on the side of the boat to retie his new-looking Sperry topsiders.

Stella said nonchalantly, "Then you might wanna head over to Cheeca Rocks. I'm pretty sure some guys were lobstering there a little while ago when I went out to gas up the boat. Looked like tourists."

It was a lie, but an effective one. Grody set his sights for Cheeca Rocks and, without another word, hammered the throttle and headed out of the channel.

The annual free-for-all known as Mini Lobster Season was two days away. Each July, the Florida Fish and Wildlife Commission opened the waters surrounding the Keys to a two-day Mini Season. It afforded recreational fisherman the chance to grab their share of the ocean's bounty before the commercial season began. But what started as a nice idea turned in to a cluster-fuck of drunks from the mainland raping the Keys. Why should Stella have to wait to share the water with those jerks? She lived there, after all. Locals should be able to harvest from the sea all year long, especially if, like her and the Petersons, they relied on their fishing skills to fill their bellies.

And really, what was the big deal? She wasn't hurting anyone. Lobstering and crabbing laws were in place just to make the government richer than it already was.

She mused over the unfairness of it all as she

filled her lungs and dove toward the sandy bottom. True, technically Mini Lobster Season didn't start for another two days, but lobstering rules should be aimed at tourists. Their pockets were lined with riches, anyway. Not Stella. Life had always been a challenge for her and she was tired of rising to the occasion.

The stirring of the silt below gave away the hidey-hole of a good catch. Stella swam deeper. She positioned herself and then crammed the tickle stick in one side of a hunk of dead coral. Out the other side swam one of the biggest Florida lobsters Stella had ever seen. Then, as if she'd willed him to do it, he flung himself right into her net. She laughed underwater, bubbles floating up, the sound ringing tinny in her ears. She pushed off the bottom and resurfaced, checking her surroundings for Dave Grody or another from his band of self-righteous do-gooders. Seeing no one, she climbed into the boat and stowed her catch in the bait well. Yes, things were going unusually well for Stella. But it had been a long time coming.

Things had really come unraveled Sunday night. She'd been scheduled to work late. Before Julie Peterson arrived to pick her up on the way to the Cholesterol Hut—the name Stella not-so-lovingly gave to the diner where they both worked—she begged Louis to take it easy on the cocktails. Matt needed to be picked up from football practice at eight o'clock. He was assistant coach to some younger players. It didn't pay a lot, but it was a decent wage for a kid his age.

"This is important, Louis. I'm counting on you."

He had nodded and continued on his way outside to sit by the dock. Stella finished getting ready for work and then went downstairs to say goodbye.

"I've gotta go, Julie's here." She bent and gave Louis a quick peck on the cheek. He barely noticed. "Please remember what I said about tonight. No drinks until you get Matt home."

"Okay, I heard you." Louis slapped the arm of his canvas chair. "Stop hounding me!"

Later that evening, Stella received a gut-wrenching text from Matt in the middle of her shift. "AT HOSPITAL WITH DAD. WE HAD AN ACCIDENT. DAD WAS DRUNK."

Stella had to tell her boss it was an emergency, which it was, and deal with his hostile comments. She always covered other people's shifts, was never late, and had been one of his hardest workers for more than five years, for wages that could make you laugh. Or cry. None of that mattered. The manager was still belittling her as she clocked out and left.

The closest hospital was only five miles north in Tavernier, but already everything was slowed down by the Mini Season early arrivals. She'd all but run out of her shift and pushed through traffic and with guns a-blazing, Stella blew through the hospital doors. Everything she'd been holding in came spilling out.

"What the hell is wrong with you?!" she shouted as soon as she'd found Louis' room.

He kept his gaze on his hands. He didn't answer. Louis blinked unfocused eyes in the slow, foggy manner of a man who spends most of his waking hours in the sauce.

Across the room, Matt sat in a turquoise pleather chair, staring at the floor like everything was somehow his fault. "We swerved off the neighborhood road on that sharp bend you always warn me about. We went off the shoulder and crashed through the mangroves. Dad hit his head on the steering wheel. They say he has a concussion. But, I'm fine."

Stella turned to Louis, who looked small and pathetic leaning into himself with his head all bandaged up, not at all the serious, steady cop she'd met nearly two decades ago. She spat out curse words until her throat was hoarse and she was sick to her stomach. Finally, when most of the initial anger was out, and said, deflated, "You're hurting us, Louis."

"Fine," he said, his defenses finally triggered. "I just pay the bills around here, but since I'm ruining everyone's life, I'll quit drinking!" He was referring to his pension from his years as a cop, which kept a roof over their head.

"When? When are you going to quit?"

"When I'm ready!"

Stella had thrown up her hands. "I swear to Christ, Louis, if you don't stop drinking *right* now, I'll kill you."

A little blood trickled down from under his bandage, bright red and between his eyes. Stella reached out with a tissue from the bedside table and wiped it away. "Christ, Louis," she said suddenly feeling beaten. "Our son could have been killed. You could have been killed."

At that moment, a young doctor in blue scrubs walked in. His toned arms and purposeful demeanor served as a stark comparison to Louis' chalky skin and swollen belly. He held some test results, and they weren't good. "Your organs are beginning to shut down, Mr. Callahan. If you don't stop drinking, you'll be dead within the year."

Stella arched one eyebrow at her husband as if to

say, "See, dumbass?"

Five hours later, Stella took home Matt, who remained withdrawn, and Louis, who wore thirteen stitches in his head. She'd been given strict instructions about how to care for Louis' concussion, including NO alcohol consumption. He was on a pretty heavy dose of pain killers and they were warned that mixing those babies with alcohol could be deadly.

When the three of them walked in the living room, Louis turned toward them and said, "I'm done drinking. Goodnight," and went to bed.

All that had happened last night. When Stella had gotten out of bed this morning, Louis had remained asleep, and that was good because it'd been a restless night for him. He'd been stiff, agitated, and altogether shaken up, which was to be expected. She knew that living without alcohol wasn't going to be easy for him, so she eliminated the temptation, dumping the contents of their liquor cabinet down the drain. She spent over an hour scouring the place, taking about fifteen half-empty bottles from over the sink, the backs of cabinets, from side table drawers and even a couple secret places in the tool room under the house that Louis didn't think she knew about. Stella was damn good at finding hidey-holes, that was just one of her gifts.

And some of the stash *was* hers, she had to admit. Although Louis kept to his Sapphire Gin, they still had other liquors in various quantities from their early years when they experimented with trendy mixed drinks. Campari, spiced rum, tequila—dumping the tequila hurt. She liked a shot of it after a long shift. And the smell of it drifting up to her as it snaked its way down the drain, caused a craving in her throat. But she was willing to do almost anything to get her husband back. Including wasting hundreds of dollars of good liquor.

She scoured the house thoroughly and silently, hoping not to wake either of her sleeping guys. She had half a thought to go through Matt's room, but he'd been up late and he needed his sleep. Plus, there'd be nothing in Matt's room for Louis to drink besides some old, red Gatorade.

Stella had pushed off the dock while Louis and Matt slept. And now, many hours later, with her bait well full of succulent lobsters and Grody off her scent, she pointed the bow toward home.

It was an uncannily calm and serene day. The water flat. Stella loved the idea of being out here on a Monday morning instead of taking breakfast orders and filling coffee cups. As she pushed the throttle and picked up speed, her hair began to whip her cheeks, and the sun warmed her. Stella felt good. Things were going to be different. Louis would change. Her marriage had another chance. And maybe Matt could remember what it was like to be part of a normal family, just in time to go off to college.

She beamed as she ran her boat through Snake Creek's no-wake zone. The water was her medication. Today she needed a lengthy dose.

A grey dorsal fin broke the glassy surface and she slowed to an idle. A mother dolphin and her young calf were heading out to the flat, calm waters of the bay.

"Hello, my beauties."

Stella leaned over the side as the mother rolled slightly to get a better look at who had greeted them. The mom was careful to prevent her calf from getting too close to the boat.

"Don't worry momma, I won't hurt your baby."

The dolphins dove and came up on the other side, exhaling loudly.

"You guys are lucky." Stella scanned the horizon before looking back at them. "You're free."

Another quick look at Stella and they were gone. She hoped they were an omen of more good things.

Her outlook momentarily soured at the sight of Betty Hodges, the eighty-year-old busybody who lived across the canal with her three-legged Chihuahua, Miss Annabelle. Stella loved animals, but she hated Miss Annabelle, who barked every time the wind blew. Betty stood on her newly bricked deck, hair teased into a massive beehive, and lips smeared with red lipstick.

"Good Morning, Neighbor!"

Stella pretended not to hear.

"Helloo! Stella!" The woman waved an emaciated arm as her dog howled in protest of the boat's proximity to its territory.

Stella nodded.

"You didn't say hello to Miss Annabelle!"

Stella rolled her eyes.

Betty scooped up her freshly groomed darling and held her close. "Miss Annabelle's been having a real doozy of a morning, haven't' you, my love?" Betty spoke loudly enough for Stella to hear over her boat's engine. "Poor little poopsie doesn't like these big waves."

Stella suddenly saw what Betty was talking about and slowed to an idle once more. The water in their canal was higher than usual, and the calm surface had quickly morphed into a swift churn. Stella looked back and her brow furrowed. Snake Creek, which had been serene and flat just minutes ago was flowing swiftly and the surface was now dark and choppy. A hurricane was set to hit far off the coast later that week but was predicted not to make landfall anywhere near the Keys. Still, she knew the ocean well enough to know some kind of storm was coming, even though the sky was still clear.

Stella took off, causing another round of piercing barks from Miss Annabelle. She made her way down the canal, careful of the rocking waves as she approached her dock. Then she saw something that made her heart sink.

Louis was at the end of the dock, asleep in his favorite stadium chair, head slumped down, a liquor bottle gleaming beside him.

She ran the boat a short way past her house and then turned around so she could lodge the side fitted with bumpers against the dock.

Then she shouted over the din of her single outboard. "What the hell do you think you're doing?"

Louis didn't stir.

"Louis! Wake up, Goddammit!"

Stella threw the bowline and made quick work of tying up. She cut the engine and stepped off onto the dock. Shaking, she walked toward him and grabbed him by the shoulder, perhaps a little more roughly than was necessary. She shouted again. "Louis! Wake up!"

Louis still didn't move.

She lifted the bottle to her nose and winced, both from the smell and from the fresh cuts on her right hand, courtesy of the lobsters. "Where the fuck did you get more gin? This isn't even your brand! Louis, I told you, if you don't cut this shit out, I'm gonna kill you."

It took Stella another few moments to realize that wouldn't be necessary. Louis was already dead.

PATTYCAKES

By the time Patty "Pattycakes" Farley was twenty-five, she'd been a bartender, bank teller, taxi driver, burger flipper, house painter, and dog sitter, all while maintaining a steady buzz. When she'd been fired yet again for drinking on the job, and her very Catholic mother had all but disowned her, she'd packed everything she had into her Volkswagen Bus and drove straight for greener pastures. She never looked twice at the cityscapes she left behind. "Good riddance, Mass-holes!" In the background, Kenny Chesney sang about life on the rock. "Paradise, here I come!"

After three days of pretty much nonstop driving, Lucille, her beloved VW, broke down in front of a waterfront bar in the Florida Keys. A forty-foot tall, wooden mermaid towered over the side of the road, indicating that she'd landed at a place called The Lorelei. It looked like something from a movie set. The open air, seaside bar was built over shallow, turquoise water. Live music and the smell of fried food beckoned. Patty'd found her new home.

She kicked off her shoes, tossed them onto the passenger seat, and called AAA on her way to the bar. The rough, sandy dirt felt heavenly, although her feet looked like they belonged to something that could swoop down from the sky and snatch its dinner from the ocean. But Patty didn't care. Bare feet were happy feet.

"What'll you have?" asked a bartender. His bleached hair and brown skin told her he spent his days off in the sun. Not bad.

"How 'bout a Miller Lite, a shot of Patrón, and a job?" Patty's signature smile spread across her face and she wondered if she'd brushed her teeth since leaving Boston.

"I can help with the first two, but you'll have to talk to the manager about the third. He's in there." The bartender pointed at a small trailer at the edge of the parking lot.

She brought the frosty bottle to her lips. It felt good. Her lips had seemed perpetually chapped from 1a lifetime spent above the Mason-Dixon Line.

"Is he cool?"

The bartender rolled his eyes. "He's a dick." Then he rushed off to wait on a group of leather-skinned geezers who looked like they were in a hurry to eat. Maybe it was so they could ingest the virtual pharmacy of prescription drugs organized in a plastic pill keeper they'd set on the table like a centerpiece.

"Perfect." She tossed back the Patrón.

It wasn't like she hadn't worked for assholes before. She knew how to handle them. Life was a game. You could play along and have fun, or fight it every step of the way and be miserable. She prided herself on knowing her limitations and never letting her ego get in the way. Some people were born to be wealthy while others were born to clean up after them. It didn't bother Patty that she was in the latter bunch. As long as she had a decent place to live, someone to fuck, and a fridge full of brews, she was satisfied.

When the AAA guy showed up an hour later, she was two beers and three shots in. He looked to be about Patty's age and although he was missing a few teeth, he wasn't that bad.

"What's wrong with this here bus?" he said in a surprisingly strong Southern drawl.

"I don't really know. The engine started making a knocking sound right before it stalled. I managed to drift to the side of the road without getting clobbered."

"Y'all here for Mini Season?" He opened the back hatch to gain access to the engine.

"What's Mini Season?"

He shook his head as he pulled out the dipstick to check the level of the oil. "Never mind. Where you headed, ma'am?"

"Don't know. Left Massachusetts just a couple days ago."

"Well, it's a dadgum miracle you made it this far," he said. "You ain't got a drop of oil in this rig."

"Are you shitting me?" Patty kicked at the dirt and laughed then whacked at a mosquito biting her lily-white thigh.

The AAA dude's head snapped in her direction at the sound of the loud slap. Then she watched him do a slow-motion double-take. Her toenails were so long they were curling over her pale piggies. And somewhere along the way, she'd developed a mysterious fungus on her big toe that she'd intended to treat, but had slipped her mind. Patty covered one bare foot with the other.

"I'll dump five or six quarts in and see what happens, but you best be fixin' to get this thing looked at right quick. Make sure this engine ain't gone cattywampus."

Ten minutes later, her VW was full of oil but it wasn't running.

"Something's wrong with the dad-burned fuel pump." He opened the hood again and rooted around. "Yep, this's beyond my pay grade, if you know what I mean. Y'all best be takin' it to a shop."

"A shop? Like a mechanic shop?"

"Yep, like a mechanic shop. There's one just yonder. Give you a tow if you'd like."

"And what sort of price would something like this run? I'm guessing AAA won't cover it."

"The tow, yes. The rest, no. You're looking at ... at least three, four hundred for parts and labor, I reckon."

"Oh fuck, I can't afford that. Can't I just camp it here in a parking lot for a couple days?"

"Well, now ma'am, I hate to be the one to break it to ya, but they're a little uppity on stuff like that 'round here, especially 'round Mini Season. Call them Lobster People. You know, people camping out in cars and such. Plus, with weather like this coming, it just plain ain't safe."

"Weather looks good to me," Patty said. And indeed, it did, it was a splendidly sunny day with a sliver of calm beach visible just beyond the bar.

"Don't be hoodwinked. News just announced a hurricane's about seventy-two hours out."

Patty pulled herself into the driver's seat and leaned an elbow out the window.

"Category 2—that's what they're saying—you don't have to skedaddle out of the county, but you'll wanna to be indoors, not in a car or mobile home or the like. Y'all have anyone here? Friends? Kin?" he asked.

"Nope. Don't know a single soul in the South."

"Then I reckon you best find a motel or something."

"Ugh, can't afford that either. Was planning to pull into town, get a job at a bar, and figure things out from there."

The AAA guy nodded. She obviously wasn't the first out-of-towner who rolled in to Islamorada with no plan. "There are buses, ma'am, you can git one of them outta here. I mean, you have options."

Options, indeed. For as long as she could remember, Patty had played a mental game of "would I fuck them" with nearly every person she met, man or woman. It made everyone seem a lot more interesting. She decided, all-in-all, the AAA guy was fuckable.

"What about you, handsome? Where are you staying?" Patty sidled her boobs up against her arm, giving him a good eyeful of her tank top-clad cleavage.

Without missing a beat, AAA guy said, "Me and the missus and our boy are hightailing it to the mainland tonight to stay with the in-laws. Just to be safe, you know? I reckon you ought to git a bus and git gone, seriously. The mainland ain't too far, and if you're low on funds, it's kind of a no-brainer."

Patty sat in Lucille a long while and took stock of her situation. Taking stock of her situation was one of her least favorite things. But she had a background feeling, something she didn't like. She wasn't afraid of weather, she'd made it through plenty of freezing New England blizzards in her bus. But blizzards didn't become floods. Plus, she'd had a working automobile then. The option to move was still hers.

She glanced around at the place she'd been ready to call her island paradise. It was exactly what she'd been hoping for—a place to idle by the ocean, rolling into work at some easy evening bartending job, sleeping late and day drinking at the water's edge. But this hurricane meant she'd have to find a real place like a motel or something—or leave. She didn't have the heart to get on a bus yet. She didn't have the heart to leave Lucille here to rot.

Three days. She had three days to sort it out or be gone.

She knocked on the door to the rusty trailer at the other end of the parking lot. A grunt from within let her know the owner was home. She turned the knob and walked up the detached set of steps.

"Hey. I'm Patty. People call me Pattycakes." She extended her hand to an overweight man sitting behind a makeshift desk. He was in need of a shave and shower and was most certainly not fuckable. The air inside was stale and humid and Patty was suddenly and powerfully reminded of the stench of her brothers' sweaty hockey gear: a mixture of armpit and crotch sweat.

He ignored Patty's outstretched hand. "Yeah? Whattaya want, Pattycakes?"

"You hiring?"

"You local?"

"Am now," she replied. "Just pulled in."

The blotchy-faced man lifted a butt cheek and farted. "Come back in six months."

"Come on, man, I'm good to go. I've bartended a ton of places."

He gave her a hard once-over. "Not interested until I know you're sticking around. Wastes time and money hiring kids who bounce out of here as soon as they get bored. Lost two just in the last couple months.

Just fucking, poof, disappeared. On to the next island."

"I'm not a kid."

He looked up, taking a long study of her. She knew what he saw: a pasty New England chick with red hair and grubby feet. She was barely thirty, but she'd been doing some hard living and she knew it showed.

"You like to drink on the job." It was a statement more than a question.

"Nope," she answered quickly. "Not me."

"Sure," he put his head down and got back to his work, which involved a stubby pencil and some musty sheets of paper.

"Look, you said you just lost some people."

"We got a Cat 3 hurricane or some shit coming in a few days. That's why I'm finishing up all this bullshit paperwork now."

"I heard it was a cat two."

"Look, sweetheart, go back to wherever you came from until this blows over. Then I'll maybe think about it."

"Can't. My car broke down."

He looked up wearily. "Then you better start walking."

Patty took his advice and walked a couple blocks over to the garage where two other guys who looked a lot like her AAA man were underneath cars. The girl in the waiting room was small with big curly black hair pinned back and she wore big gold hoop earrings that were turning green on the inside. She snapped pink bubblegum like the unabashed cliché she was. The chipped and stained nametag on her ample bosom announced to the world that her name was Belinda. Oh well, thought Patty, I'm a cliché too. Might as well embrace it.

She asked the girl if they'd be open the following day and how long it would take to replace a fuel pump. Belinda called out to someone in the back and he came in wiping his dirty hands and said, in as many words, no way in hell that's happening before the storm. Patty pitched her most desperate plea, told them she was stranded, her only vehicle would be demolished, which happened to also be her only home. The mechanic checked his watch. His mustache twitched, he looked a little flustered. He was probably another family man, thought Patty, trying to do right by the little lady. Fuckable, yes. Counter wench. No. Well, yes. Under different circumstances, definitely.

"You're damned lucky. We got one of those buses back home, junked for parts, sitting in the backyard. If you really need it, I'll put it in tonight. You gotta tow?"

"Nope, but I can get one."

"Okay, get it over here as soon as you can. We're staying open two more days for stuff like this, but closing up early, so be here to pick it up by 3:00 pm day after tomorrow."

"What'll it cost?"

He took of the small specs he was wearing and blew on them, wiping them with the one clean edge of his hanky.

"If it's what you say it is, around three hundred."

Patty's heart sank, but she nodded.

Did she have a choice? The idea of finding a bus stop and hightailing it up to some gymnasium in Miami-Dade and leaving poor Lucille behind made her sick to her stomach. Just real sick. And then what? Still out of money, but with no car. If she could just make some real money tonight, it would solve all her problems. She'd get some money, get Lucille fixed, and then get out of Dodge before the storm.

"Where's cheap to stay around here?" she asked Belinda the Counter Girl. The mechanic had gone back to the garage as soon as Patty had nodded to his terms.

"Cheapest you could find is like two hundred a night because it's Mini Season. But IDK, maybe people are canceling their reservations cuz of the storm."

The way she said "two hundred" in her nasal way made it clear that Belinda the Counter Girl didn't think Pattycakes had two hundred dollars to her name. And she would be correct.

"What the hell *is* Mini Season?"

"Hello?" Behind Patty an older couple came in, jangling the little bell at the top of the door and nodding anxiously to Belinda. They looked to be in their late sixties, probably there to pick up their car and get out of town, ahead of the storm. Belinda summarily dismissed Pattycakes, calling the customers by name and assuring them Don was just finishing up on their Volvo but he'd been "interrupted."

Patty rolled her eyes. Three hours in paradise and so far everyone either hated her or pitied her.

She called AAA and arranged for a tow from The Lorelei. Then she stuffed her sleeping bag and a couple changes of clothes into her duffel bag and stashed it in some scrub behind a big scraggy tree in the Lorelei parking lot.

Patty waited at the bar with a couple cold Miller Lites, suddenly realizing her stomach demanded nutrition that didn't come from a beer can. She wanted to use the last of her money wisely; who knew how far she'd have to stretch it. Twenty dollars of it would cover either a plate of fish tacos and a shot of tequila at the Lorelei, or a convenience store six-pack and some junk food.

She told the hot bartender her sad story. He was busy and mostly indifferent, but a scrubby, sinewy guy who sat near her at the bar looked her way. He downed a couple shots in quick succession, cocked his head in her direction, and said: "Try The Snatch Patch. Less than half a mile down the road. Sam'll take care of you."

"The Snatch Patch? Is that what I think it is?"

"You bet your sweet ass."

"I'm not a stripper, I'm a mixologist."

The bartender looked up from the mojito he was making. "Bartenders aren't nude, they just have to go topless. But I hear they make good money."

Patty was about to ask more questions when the AAA tow truck showed up outside.

She groaned and left the bar. A greying chubby guy latched up Lucille with a grunt and hauled her the two blocks without really saying much to Patty. Definitely not fuckable.

After signing papers and checking Lucille in to her new home at the auto shop, she took a deep breath. She was officially homeless. And hungry. And she had to pee. Belinda the Counter Girl said the shop bathroom was occupied. Patty waited, and waited, but it seemed like whoever was in there was taking forever.

Across from the garage was a shitty-looking little convenience store called the Tom Thumb. Its lot was knee-deep in cars, strange for a Monday evening, at least where Patty was from. Maybe this was the early hurricane freak-out. Had to be. A line of pickup trucks towed trailered boats of all shapes and sizes. She guessed these people were on their way out of town like everyone else.

The three beers she'd had back at the Lorelei were passing right through her. Patty hurried through the door of the Tom Thumb, crashing into a truly hideous woman with bleach blond hair and ill-fitting leopard print leggings. They both hit the deck. Leopard Print screeched "Ex-CUUUSE ME!" as she scrambled to pick up the handful of items that had fallen from her bag. It was an annoying accent Patty recognized. Long Island or New Jersey. You can't get away from Northeastern assholes, no matter how far you go. Leopard Print was carrying a plastic bag with three bottles of Poland Spring, a loaf of Wonder Bread, and tucked underneath, unmistakable, a sweaty six pack of Miller Lite. She crammed the waters and the bread back into the flimsy plastic grocery bag and thundered off without giving Patty a second look. The collision had surprised her more than Leopard Print, and being a bit tipsy had made it more challenging for Patty to get up in one go.

Someone approached from behind and offered a hand to help her off the floor.

"Thanks," she said, steadying herself. "But I'm good."

The man smiled. Patty headed straight for the restroom, but found the ladies' room door locked. After only a moment's hesitation, she tried the men's room, but found that locked, too. FOR PAYING CUSTOMERS ONLY.

"Shit!" Patty assessed the long line of impatient customers waiting to check out. She decided to grab some beer and snacks and get the bathroom key ASAP.

The beer cooler was nearly empty. The only choices left were Natty Light and Bud. She stomped her foot but that only agitated her bladder more.

"Slim pickings, huh?" The man who'd offered to help her off the floor stood beside her, looking as disappointed as she felt. "You'd think these places would stock up for Mini Season, right? And now with the hurricane—well, I guess people gotta find something to do when they're stuck inside."

"Oh my God," groaned Patty. "Mini Season. Hurricane. Which one is it? Are people coming or going?"

"Ha," the man gave her a genuine laugh. "That's Islamorada for you. The place where no one wants to be—and everyone wants to be—simultaneously."

"Yeah, well, it's been a stressful fucking day, and I just want a Miller Lite."

"Ditto."

Patty shifted her weight from leg to leg. "Crap, I gotta pee."

"Don't panic." The man turned his head toward the front of the store and shouted. "Hey, Carlos! This lady wants Miller Lite. You got any in the back?"

"Oh, you didn't have to do that!" She waved it off, but smiled at the gesture.

"What you see is what we got, Hammond," shouted the cashier. "Last six-pack just walked out the door."

"That New Jersey devil!" Patty laughed, trying to sound as upbeat as she normally felt. "Thanks for trying. Hammond, is it?"

The man stuck out his hand. As Patty shook it, he answered, "Yeah. Chris Hammond. And Mini Season is just a two-day fishing season open to the public before the commercial boats come in. You can get yourself some good lobster. It's a big deal down here. Lots of tourists. Only happens once a year."

"Oh yeah? And a hurricane's hitting at the same time, so they all have to turn around and go home. Hah!" She gave that a genuine laugh.

"Seems like," Hammond had a nice smile and he offered it to her. "By the way, what's your name, Darlin'?"

He said "Darling" in a nice way, with a soft twang. Nothing creepy about it, not that Patty usually minded creepy.

"Patty. People called me Pattycakes."

"So, you blow into town just around the same time as your namesake. Huh, must be something to that."

"Namesake?"

"Hurricane Patty."

"You gotta be shitting me."

They stood in line while Hammond made small talk about growing up on the island. Patty's pee-pee dance became less and less subtle. But when he mentioned being in law enforcement, her overloaded bladder was momentarily forgotten.

"You're a cop?"

"I prefer police officer, but yeah. Why?"

Patty shook her head. "Because you seem nice. Cops are dicks."

Hammond laughed. "I suppose some of us are, but not all. Just like not all Irish women are mean drunks."

It was Patty's turn to laugh. "You're wrong about that!"

She was buzzed, and the idea of banging a cop was

very appealing, even though he looked about fifteen years her senior and had a beer belly. He wasn't wearing a wedding ring, and he was definitely fuckable.

"Hey, you wanna have a drink with me?"

Hammond looked uncomfortable.

Immediately Patty started to back-peddle. "Hey, no biggie. I just remembered I have to work tonight, anyway. See ya."

She paid for her Natty Lite, a can of Pringles, and a bag of Combos, and then bolted from the counter, red-faced and embarrassed. She was so anxious to get out of the suddenly claustrophobic convenience store that she forgot to ask for the bathroom key.

Patty high-tailed it to a far corner of the parking lot. She knew she'd never make it back to the Lorelei without pissing her pants. She rested her back against a low ledge and squatted between two cars. The first dribbles forced their way out, dampening her underwear before she could even get it all the way down.

"Was it something I said?"

"Jesus Christ!" Patty startled, losing her balance and peeing all over her shorts and down her leg. It was impossible to stop the flow.

The man laughed and turned his back as she pulled up her pants. "Marking your territory?"

Jesus. It was the cop she'd just asked out. She was mortified.

"Give a girl some privacy, would ya?"

She grabbed her bags and tried to sneak away, but Hammond turned and called to her. "Hey, wait a minute!" He caught up to her, careful to step around the puddle she'd left on the blacktop.

"Am I under arrest?"

"You ran away too quickly for me to answer. I'm married, so I just need to put that out there. But since you're new in town, I'd be happy to meet up with you sometime tomorrow evening and help you get situated for the storm."

"Cool, Hoss," Patty said, trying to be nonchalant while acutely aware of her the wet spot on her pants. "I'll take you up on that offer."

"Great. How about we meet at Hog Heaven tomorrow around 9:00 pm?"

Patty hesitated. Things were getting stressful. She wanted a little time with him before she left, but she needed to make some real money before then, too. She wondered if she could do both.

"I don't know that place. Can we make it The Lorelei?"

"Sure."

Patty thought he looked a bit self-conscious, avoiding too much eye contact. That was a good thing. Maybe that meant he thought she was fuckable. And he would be right.

She aimed a finger snap at his chest. "Cool. See you there, Hoss."

"Hey, Darlin," he called out as she staggered away. "You okay walking by yourself?"

"No worries." She waved her hand dismissively, hoping she looked casual. Inside her chest, though, her heart thumped as if trying to make a break for it. No one had ever called her Darlin' like that, and she liked it. It wasn't condescending, just nice, companionable. And a little more than companionable. Her nether region had something to say about it.

Patty was now in the proper frame of mind for an interview at The Snatch Patch.

*B*ART

Bart Levine woke in a terrible state. The sofa beneath him was soaked with sweat. Stumbling to the cramped kitchen reeking with weeks' old dirty dishes, he opened the fridge and settled for a cold beer for breakfast. He was out of everything he needed, except beer. His hands shook as he pulled the top, but he was used to it.

He staggered out the back door and plopped down on cement steps that led to a bare yard enclosed by a rusty chain link fence. The afternoon sun was intense. Sweat dripped from his scalp and down his forehead. Bart sat motionless, watching an iguana perched on a pile of broken cinder blocks at the end of the drive. He thought about how different his childhood backyard had been from the dismal, arid patch of nothing surrounding the concrete house.

Bart was in his late thirties and never owned a car or held a steady job. He didn't have a bank account or a credit card. He liked to think he was a ladies' man, but his only real talent in life was getting wasted. His current situation involved sleeping on a cousin's sofa in Homestead and pushing meth to neighborhood kids. It wasn't a very profitable venture for Bart, because he smoked, snorted, and swallowed about as much as he sold.

Draining the beer that had already grown warm,

Bart stood and pissed off the steps, trying to arch the stream far enough to hit the sunning lizard. It never flinched.

Back inside, he tossed the empty into the sink and grabbed another as his cousin walked in the front door.

"You look like shit." His older cousin, Tiny, weighed over 300 pounds and stood a foot taller than Bart. Tiny said what he wanted and did what he wanted, and Bart had just learned to live with it.

"Got anything?"

"Fresh out, Cuz'. But you gotta get cleaned up because I gotta job for you. Right up your alley."

Bart eyed him quizzically. No job was "up his alley" unless it was a blow job.

"Some chick got fucked up in a car accident a few months ago. She's been in rehab at Jackson Memorial and is gettin' released today. Needs a ride back to her a trailer park in Islamorada."

"So why don't she get a cab?"

"Cuz her car is sitting in the parking garage at the hospital. Easy money, man. You in?"

"Since when do I drive a fuckin' Uber?"

"Since you owe me, you good-for-nothing piece of shit."

Bart averted his eyes, but still felt shitty enough to challenge Tiny. "Why ain't you doin' it?"

"Gotta do something for Sam."

Bart considered how nice it would be to get out of Tiny's filthy house and just drive. He hoped the bitch would be looped on painkillers and not talk too much. Nothing he hated more than a broad that never shut up.

"How'm I supposed to get there?"

"I'll drop you off, you dumbass."

"And how am I getting back?"

"She'll pay your cab fare back. It's a freakin' no-brainer. You'll do it."

Bart nodded vacantly.

"Good, 'cuz I told her you'd be there an hour ago."

Tiny dropped his cousin off at the main entrance to Jackson Memorial and pulled away without a word. Bart went to the registration desk to find the old lady whose name Tiny had scribbled on the back of a taco wrapper. A slender woman stood behind the counter, shuffling clipboards and manila folders.

"Hey, I'm here to pick up . . . Emma Hinkley?" The name scribbled on the wrapper was hard for Bart to sound out. Reading had never been his strong suit. The woman behind the counter didn't bother to reply, she just pointed to his right before turning to answer the phone. Uppity bitch. Could use a stiff one up her ass. Teach her some manners.

To his right he saw a couple of old men slumped in plastic waiting-room-style chairs. The seats were joined at the armrest, forcing the occupants to jockey for the use of it. Near them sat a woman in the tightest spandex leggings Bart had ever seen. They were a few sizes too small and forced a generously-sized fat roll to escape over the waistband and hang down below her crotch. He didn't mind a few curves on a woman—no one liked to bang a skeleton—but even he had limits.

He waited until the snotty desk chick was off the phone before asking again. "Which one's Emma Hinkley?

"I am," said a voice to his right. It came from a chick in a wheelchair. She looked a little rough, but considering she'd been in a bad wreck and had spent months lying in a hospital bed, Bart didn't think she looked too bad. With a few good meals and some sun, he might even bang her.

"You ready to bust outta this joint, or what?"

"Hell yeah!" She dug through a bag in her lap and held out a set of keys. "My car's in the garage. Get me outta this shit hole!"

The nurse behind the counter scowled at them and Bart and Emma laughed.

He pushed her chair to the elevators, catching a whiff of something unpleasant when they passed a block of rooms. It reminded him of the nursing home when he used to visit his grandfather. The smell would never leave his memory: a sad combination of piss, stale air, and loneliness. It made his stomach turn, and the nausea that had been creeping in the background all morning came forward in full force.

They took the elevator to the second floor of a parking garage where Emma directed him to an ancient Honda. The front passenger door was painted slate grey, although the rest of the car was army green. The back window was cracked from one corner to the other, but whatever accident had left this chick in a wheelchair had done more damage to her than to the car. Bart left his charge by the passenger side and walked around the wheelchair to open the door. Movement caught his eye. He looked over his shoulder and watched Emma's face twist into a frightened grimace. Her wheelchair rolled backwards down the ramp, toward the bowels of the parking garage.

"Oh my God!" Emma grabbed at the wheels. "Help me!"

Bart lurched forward and sprinted toward the runaway chair as it gained momentum and rolled away at a good clip. He was close to catching it just as it smashed into the front end of a freshly waxed Mercedes. The impact was so hard that Bart heard the air forced from Emma's lungs just before her head flew backwards. The driver hollered from his open window. Bart's Spanish wasn't very good, but it was clear that the man wasn't inviting them out for cocktails.

"Jesus Christ! You okay?" Bart pulled the chair from the grip of the idling car.

"What the fuck do you think?"

Bart's mouth opened, but no words came out.

"Take me home without killing me, if you think you can manage it."

Bart figured he had that coming, so rather than slapping her like he wanted to, he pushed the chair to the rusty Honda and waited for Emma to get out.

"Hey Einstein," she hissed, "you *do* realize my legs are paralyzed, right? You actually have to lift me out of this piece of shit wheelchair and put me in the car."

"You can't walk?"

"Do you think I tool around in this thing just for shits and giggles?"

"Okay, geez. Hold your wad, lady. I didn't know you couldn't walk. I thought hospitals made everyone leave in a wheelchair. That's how they do it on TV."

Bart paused as if that was a reasonable explanation for his confusion.

Emma didn't look impressed, but she conceded. "I'm sorry. I need a drink. If you buy me a bottle of Jack, I'll pay you extra. I haven't had a drink in four months." Emma closed her eyes and licked her lips.

"Four months? Shit," Bart said. "You must be miserable. I can't go four hours."

With a little guidance, Bart scooped the small-framed woman from the wheelchair and arranged her on the stained front seat. She flinched at his touch and Bart wondered how long it had been since someone other than a doctor or nurse had laid hands on her. Emma's tense body leaned away from him and her intimidation made him feel powerful.

A few blocks from the hospital, Bart pulled into the parking lot of a liquor store. The bars on the windows were a testament to the quality of the neighborhood. "Will you be okay out here while I run in for the Jack?" Considering he'd almost killed her moments before, he thought he should at least act like he cared.

She looked at Bart and scowled. "I'll be fine."

As he waited in line cradling the booze in the crook of his arm, Bart watched Emma through the bulletproof glass. She pulled down the visor and assessed her reflection in the mirror. She ran her hands through her hair and then pinched her cheeks. He watched as she pulled something from her purse and applied it to her lips. Her primping made him laugh. Chicks were all the same. Vain and horny.

Bart paid and walked out into Miami's relentless heat. He handed Emma the bottle, which she opened before he could get the old Honda in gear. She put the bottle to her lips and took a long pull. Bart laughed. "Thirsty, Crip?"

"I plan to be shitfaced by the time we get to Jewfish Creek."

"Everyone needs a goal." He considered hers a lofty one. "Mind if I take a sip? I drive better with a buzz."

"Nobody drives better with a buzz." She passed him the bottle.

True to her word, by the time Bart managed to weave Emma's decrepit Honda over the last bridge before landing in Key Largo, she was well on her way to being hammered. Bart was enjoying himself. While classic rock blared out of the cracked speakers on the bleached-out dash, they passed the bottle back and forth, slipping into a comfortable state of numb.

Emma turned down the radio. "I was hoping to make it home, but this fucking traffic is slowing us down. I'm about to piss my pants. We gotta stop."

"No prob. Just tell me where."

"Hang a left." She pointed with her elbow. Her hands held the bottle of Jack and she seemed reluctant to put it down. "There's a bar back there."

"Twist my arm!" Bart followed Emma's directions and eventually parked in a mostly shady spot in front of what looked like a ranch-style home backed up to a marina. He hopped out and opened the passenger door. "How 'bout we forget the wheelchair? I'll just carry you, plop you on the shitter, and wait outside the door until you need me. It's easier to carry you than to push the damn thing anyway."

Emma shrugged, happy and buzzed. "Whatever you say." Carefully cradled in Bart's arms, she directed him through the bar and to the ladies room.

Bart pushed open a stall door with his boot. "Um, do I just put you on the john and leave or . . . do you need help with your drawers?"

Emma was drunk enough to giggle. She pushed

her yoga pants and underwear down over her hips, exposing herself to Bart who didn't have the decency to look away.

"Put me on the toilet and I'll tell you when I'm done."

He positioned her as carefully as he could and then backed out, closing the stall door behind him. Emma laughed again. "I guess this wasn't what you were expecting, huh?"

"Not really, but it's cool." Bart busied himself posing like a body builder in front of the mirror until Emma called for him. Like a seasoned pro, he bent at the waist and pulled her off the toilet. He leaned her over his right shoulder while he pulled up her undies and yoga pants. He got a good look at her bush while doing so and decided that with a shower and shave, she'd be a decent lay. He felt a tingle in his shorts, but dismissed it. His pecker would have to wait.

Bart had difficulty maneuvering back to the car with Emma in his arms. She was too drunk to notice, however, and was snoring by the time he positioned her in the front seat.

The shots of Jack bolstered Bart's bravado. He lifted Emma's shirt while she slept.

"Just checking to see what's under the hood." He pulled one nipple until it stiffened into a hard peak. "Oh yeah, I'm gonna fuck the shit outta you for sure."

He rearranged her clothes and crawled into the driver's seat.

Enna was passed out and he didn't know where she lived, so there was really only one option.

Bart pulled into a busy waterside bar, one he almost never went to because the drinks were watered-down and pricey, and it was predictably full of tourists. He tugged a fifty from Emma's wallet and went inside.

He put the bill down on the bar and ordered three shots of good whiskey.

The bartender poured and then moved on to a red-headed chick who plopped herself on a stool a few seats down. She ordered a beer and immediately began talking the bartender's ear off about her problems: broken down VW with a hurricane on the way, how she needed a job.

Mostly just to shut her up, and because he was having a good day, Bart told her to try The Snatch Patch. Tiny bounced there sometimes, and had said they were low on bartenders lately.

When the red-head was gone, Bart asked the bartender about the hurricane.

"Gonna make landfall in a day or two," the bartended replied. "Looks like it could be a bad one."

Bart ordered himself another shot and raised it above his head. "Here's to drinkin' today and getting' the fuck out tomorrow."

Bart was getting plastered, but he didn't want to fuck things up with Emma just yet, so he made his way back to the car. She was still dead asleep. He pinched her arm and she woke.

"How much farther?" he said.

"Oh shit, I must have passed out." She sat up and looked around. "We're at The Lorelei, so I'm right around the corner." She turned to him, still groggy. "I can't wait to sleep in my own bed. If I had to spend one more night in that goddamned hospital, I'd have jumped out the window."

Bart laughed. "You can't walk, remember? How you gonna jump?"

Emma rolled her eyes. "You know what I mean, Einstein."

Bart pulled out onto the main drag, and Emma popped in a CD and hummed along with Don Henley as he crooned about the boys of summer. Emma closed her eyes, leaned out the window, and sang, "You got your hair combed back and your sunglasses on, baby . . ."

Bart swiped a big swig of Jack while she wasn't looking, grateful for the effect music had on women.

Finally, Emma pulled her head back inside the Honda. "Turn here. Last trailer on the right."

Bart pulled into the drive of a cream-colored single-wide with a redwood deck and matching shutters shaped like palm trees. The yard was full of tall weeds and fallen palm fronds, but considering the place had been vacant for four months, it didn't look too bad.

Bart's opinion changed when he unlocked the front door and was hit with a nauseating wave of rotting garbage. He backed out and emptied the contents of his stomach over the rail.

"What's wrong?" Emma hollered from the front seat. It was hard to hear over the rain that suddenly came flooding from the sky.

Bart wiped his mouth on his sleeve and hollered. "I'm all right, just wasn't' expecting that. Be right back."

He pulled off his shirt and tied it around his nose and mouth. Bart didn't think a dead, rotting body could stink up Emma's trailer any worse than four-month-old garbage. He raced inside, snatched the garbage bag from the can, and ran for the door while holding his breath. After cramming it into a street-side can, he hollered towards the car.

"Lemme open some windows and wash my hands. Then I'll come back to get you."

When he returned, sucking in clean air, Bart noticed that Emma couldn't keep her eyes off his bare chest. He carried her over the threshold of the trailer like a groom with his new bride. As he stepped inside, he farted. "Better out than in, I always say!" he laughed. "How about a drink to welcome you home, Crip?"

"My hero!" Emma pressed her mouth to his and sent her tongue on a reconnaissance mission. She was obviously tired of waiting, and Bart was only too happy to oblige.

$STELLA$

Stella Callahan whispered to a dead man: "You stupid ass."

Twenty-two years ago, she'd been in love. Sort of. A single mom, living on credit cards soon to be maxed out, she'd waited on a man old enough to be her father during a late-night waitressing shift at all-night diner in St Pete. He wasn't particularly handsome, but his hair was thick and wavy and he smelled nice. Nothing overpowering. Like old-fashioned soap and talcum powder. One look at his hands and Stella knew the customer wasn't an hourly laborer: his fingernails were clean and well-manicured. After a few dates, she convinced herself that a life with him would be better than one without. And in spite of their twenty-year age difference, Stella believed they had enough in common to carve out a happy life. Six months later, Louis and Stella were married by a Justice of the Peace. No family or friends were invited; the JP served as both officiate and witness. The newly married couple celebrated at home with cocktails.

By the time Stella realized that Louis had a drinking problem, she told herself it was no big deal. At least Matt had a father now.

Matt.

Stella felt nauseous. How was she going to tell her

son?

The coo of a nesting dove yanked Stella from her melancholy thoughts. She didn't want Matt to see his step-father sitting lifelessly on the dock. That shouldn't be his final memory.

"Christ, Louis, you're freaking dead and I still have to cover up for you." She tried to swallow the lump in her throat, but it wouldn't budge. Like a rock sitting on her windpipe.

Stella looked at the boat, which held a most delicious catch, and then at her dead husband. Her plan had been to collect the lobsters into a cooler, cover them with ice, and then grill them later when Matt got home from practice. They both loved lobsters split in half, grilled in their shells, and slathered with lots of butter and garlic. She almost decided to leave Louis sitting there while she got the lobsters inside before they died, but guilt and shame led her to abandon them. She begrudgingly turned her back on the boat. And Louis.

A minute later, Stella stood under a vent in her kitchen and dialed three digits, calmed somewhat by the cool air blowing on the back of her neck. At least the neighbors would have something to talk about.

"9-1-1, what's your emergency?"

"My husband's dead."

The operator asked for more information.

"I don't know. I guess his liver finally told him to fuck off."

"Okay," said the operator. "Help is on the way."

Stella headed to the bedroom. The overwhelming stench of morning urine from the adjoining bathroom threatened to gag her. In typical fashion, Louis had neglected to flush. She flushed for him, for the thousandth—and last—time. She stripped out of her wetsuit and then hung it in the shower to dry. She felt a sharp pain in her hand and remembered that she had some cuts from her morning expedition. She cleaned them out and fixed them up with a little iodine. She was about to get dressed, digging through a laundry basket, when she heard a soft knock on the door.

"Mom?"

Oh shit. He's home early.

"Hold on," she called. "I'll be right out."

Stella pulled on a pair of shorts and a tank top, splashed her face with water, and ran a brush through her wet, tangled hair. The mirror showed a woman who looked much older than Stella felt, but then again, the mirror had never been kind. Bags under the eyes, wrinkles around her mouth, and a saggy chicken neck. Curses passed down from her mother, God rest her soul.

Stella willed herself to be strong. In the kitchen Matt was blending bananas and mangoes for a smoothie. In spite of his height and muscular frame, Stella saw her baby. He might look like a man, but he was still a kid. One she wished she could protect forever.

"Hey, Honey." She wrapped an arm around him. "You're home from practice early."

"Yeah," he said.

She held onto him, held onto this final moment when Matt still had his father. Or thought he did.

"Was it a good practice today? How's coach's knee?"

"His knee? Oh, yeah, he's fine. Like it never bothered him."

"He give you a ride today?"

"Nope. I rode my bike." Matt pushed the blend button and the mixer made a terribly loud noise. Stella knew she was stalling for time. The cops would be on their way and she had to tell Matt the truth before they arrived.

She waited until the blender stopped.

"Honey, I'm not sure how to tell you this." She rested her head on his shoulder.

"You finally quit your job?"

Stella smiled but her heart hurt. "I wish."

Matt poured his smoothie into a tall glass tumbler.

"Matt, your Dad . . . well, you know he was very proud of you, right?"

Matt looked down at her. "Was?"

She swallowed hard around that damned lump. She was not going to cry. No way.

"What's wrong?"

"Matt, Louis is dead."

Everything was suddenly very quiet except for the sound from the struggling air conditioner.

Stella wrapped both arms around her son who stood stiff and awkward, still processing her words.

The front door clapped open. "Yo! It's Nikki!"

Stella rubbed her tired eyes with one hand and kept the other clamped around her son's waist.

Suddenly Nikki, a woman from a neighboring trailer park, thundered into the house like she owned it. "Morning, neighbor. There's a meat wagon coming down the road! Wonder who died."

"Are you okay, Mom?" whispered Matt.

Stella nodded and gave a weak smile.

"What's going on?" asked Nikki, squeezing into a chair at the kitchen table. She wore her usual leopard print leggings and black tank top two sizes too small.

The doorbell rang. "I'll explain later. Right now, I've gotta deal with the paramedics. You both stay here."

Matt stood in front of her. "I'm not a little kid anymore, Mom. I'm coming with you."

"Matt, your mom is right. You stay put!" Nikki held up her beefy hands like an elementary school crossing guard.

"Fuck you, Nikki! Nobody asked you." Matt's dislike for Nikki was always palpable, but this was the first time he'd cursed at her. He brushed past both Stella and Nikki to the front door.

"Matt! Please don't talk to Nikki that way."

Nikki put on her famous "I told you so" face, the one that made her especially hard to like. "He's not too old for a spanking."

The paramedics had circled around the house and gone straight for the dock. Stella hustled outside to catch up with Matt before he saw too much, but she was too late.

Matt was already standing with the paramedics near Louis' dead body. No one seemed to notice it had started to sprinkle. "Don't come any closer," one of them said to her son.

"What's going on?" Nikki ambled out. "I watch all the CSI shows. You want pictures? I have a camera!"

"The best way for you to help, ma'am, is to take Mrs. Callahan and her boy inside to wait for the police."

Matt flinched when the paramedic called him a boy.

"Don't worry. I'll keep them out of your hair. What are we looking at? Homicide? Suicide?"

The paramedics turned their backs on Nikki and ignored her. Stella wanted Matt inside too, so she took his arm and turned him back toward the house. Nikki ran ahead and led the trio up the back steps, gasping for air as she climbed. "My thighs are chafing! Can't you crank the air conditioning a little more, Stell? It's hotter than hell today."

Stella didn't reply. She stood in the kitchen under the air vent while Nikki did what came naturally. She ran her mouth and took charge. "Okay, first things first. Stell, did you kill Louis?"

Stella watched Matt disappear down the hall toward his bedroom. His door slammed against, Nikki, Stella, the paramedics, the whole horrible situation. She wanted to go be with him, but she knew he needed some time alone.

"Of course not, Nikki. How could you even ask me that?"

"I'm your friend. You can tell me." Nikki spoke lowly, conspiratorially. "Were you finally sick and tired of the drinking and you took him out?"

Stella stomped her foot. "Nikki! I didn't kill my husband!"

"Look, I'm just helping you practice for the coppers, 'cuz believe me, they're gonna ask you the same questions."

Stella didn't say anything. She was hot, dizzy, and distracted by the hot pink lipstick smear on her friend's front teeth.

"You should practice your story."

Stella ran her hands through her damp hair. "Story? What story? There is no story, Nikki! When I left, Louis was asleep in bed. When I came home he was dead on the dock. There's nothing more to say!"

"You aren't very credible, you know. I mean, if my

husband died, I'd be face down in a puddle of tears."

"You don't know that, Nikki. Your husband left you before he could die." Stella turned away from her friend and spoke more quietly. "You have no idea what you'd do."

"That's a low blow, Stell. All I'm saying is that if you want the cops to believe you had nothing to do with Louis' death, you need to look devastated. You aren't even crying, for Christ's sake." Nikki chewed on a fingernail. "You look guilty, if you ask me."

A part of Stella wondered if Nikki might be right: that it was weird she wasn't crying. "I'm so confused right now, I can't fucking think straight."

"Well, I'd suggest you get your head screwed on before they interrogate you." Nikki clapped her hands together and her eyes grew wide. "Oh, and we better check for evidence before the cops begin their search. I'll tell you what they're gonna do: they'll interview us, asking the same questions over and over until we crack. Then they'll search the house for pubic hairs and dried sperm."

Stella held out her hands, signaling for her friend to shut up. "Pubic hairs and sperm? That's what the cops are gonna look for? My husband died outside, but pubic hairs and sperm inside the house will be the focus of the investigation? Jesus, Nikki, you watch too much TV."

"Fine, don't believe me, but I'm telling you; it always comes down to sperm and pubes."

Stella plopped down in a chair. "Well, then they're going to be disappointed because Louis hasn't blown his wad in years."

Nikki pulled out her cell. Stella stood and yanked it

from her grasp. "Don't even think about telling anyone that or I'll kill you with my bare hands!"

"Help!" Nikki yelped, scrambling to snatch her phone back. "She's already planning to murder again!"

Stella couldn't take one more moment cooped up inside with her friend. She suggested Nikki put together some lunch, saying she was going to go check on Matt. Then Stella sidled out the front door and around the side of the house to the back yard.

A fresh cluster of cops arrived and hovered around Louis' body.

Officer Lopez, who Stella knew to be a really even-keel guy, sounded irritated. "Haven't I told you guys a thousand times to separate the witnesses?"

"Sorry, man." The paramedic shrugged. "That's your job. At least we got them away from the body."

The paramedics confirmed the man was indeed dead and left without much more to say. Stella felt like she was a watching a movie, it was all so surreal to hear her husband confirmed dead.

Lopez's partner Williamson, a greying man with a square jaw, covered Louis and the chair he died in with a black tarp. As he worked to cover large portions of the surrounding yard with other tarps, he spoke to Lopez in a flat, even tone. "Wife comes back from the boat and finds husband dead. Calls 9-1-1. Paramedics say this man has a concussion and drank enough of this bottle of gin to do himself in. Everyone knows this man was a drunk. Sounds pretty open and shut."

Lopez began snapping photos. "We'll see what the tox reports say."

Williamson pulled out his radio. "Hey, Boss. Any idea who's the coroner on duty?" Williamson nodded a few times, said thanks, and hung up.

"Coroner on duty is a moron. I'm gonna call Nichols."

Lopez kept snapping photos. "Every time, Williamson. You love yourself some Jody Nichols."

Williamson ignored him and rang another number.

"Hey buddy, where are you? Got a dead one here with your name written all over it."

He paused while the man on the other end answered.

Williamson looked irritated. "I don't care. You start slacking on the job, Nichols, and I'll be sure my boss knows. 136 Stromboli Drive in Venetian Shores."

Williamson hung up, telling Lopez he was confident that his pal would soon be along. "He talks a good game about showing up when he's damn good and ready, but the truth is Jody Nichols loves dead people." Williamson pulled on a pair of blue nitrile gloves and picked up the gin bottle sitting next to the body. He dropped it into a clear plastic bag.

"You check the body yet?" Williamson asked.

"No, was leaving that for you. After all these years, I know how much you love feeling up dead guys, just like your friend."

"Go fuck yourself, Lopez."

Juan Lopez laughed as he looked through the digital photos he'd just taken.

"Pix are spot-on for a one-handed wonder like me."

Stella felt a pang of sympathy. She knew his camera skills were lacking since he'd been in a car accident while off duty a couple months back. Some chick, high as a kite, had flown through an intersection, clipping Lopez back against a cement wall and knocking him unconscious. Lopez had been all right except his left hand, of all things, which had developed a slight tremor. If he'd been hit in his shooting hand, he'd have been off the force without a way to support his five kids and pregnant wife. As for the woman, her car had spun out and crashed. Word was she couldn't even walk anymore.

"Nichol's be here as soon as he figures out how to tell his old lady their lunch date is over," Williamson said. "Last thing that fat boy needs is another steak, anyway."

Lopez rolled his eyes and checked his watch. "He'd better hurry. After we get the body out of here and finish establishing the crime scene, let's talk to the neighbors. Somebody had to see or hear something."

"Don't bet on it, partner. Half of the senior citizens in this neighborhood are deaf and the other half are blind. Wouldn't surprise me if nobody knows nothin'."

"You're a real fucking ray of sunshine. Anyone ever tell you that, Williamson?"

Williamson just laughed. "I tell it like it is."

Stella knew it wouldn't be long until Nikki came looking for her. From her hiding place in the storage area under the deck, she watched Lopez and Williamson stake the entire yard, front and back, with yellow crime scene tape. When they were finished, the two men huddled under a group of palm trees as they waited for the coroner and radioed for a detail of officers to report to keep the crime scene clean. The wind had picked up, the Conch Republic flag flying above the Callahan's dock cracked in the wind. The accompanying rain was falling harder than before. So much for the nice day.

"How are the kids?" Williamson asked.

Lopez glanced sideways at his partner. "Growing like weeds, man, all five of them. Giancarlo is going to be eight next month, if you can believe it. Says he wants to be an officer like his old man."

"My son used to say that, too, at his age. Not anymore. Now he seems to think I'm stupid. Knows better than me. Both my kids do."

"That's teenagers for you. We were the same," Lopez said. "Hell, it wasn't until I became a father that I realized how smart my *papi* was. Probably will be the same with yours."

Williamson shrugged. "Maybe, but it irritates the shit outta me." Then he nodded, looking palpably relieved. "Nichols is here."

The coroner pulled onto the grass and then lumbered from the cool, air conditioning of his new Lexus into the warm rain.

"You ole boys napping?" In spite of the drizzle and oppressive humidity, Jody Nichols looked cool and freshly dressed.

"God knows we had enough time to fall asleep waiting for you to get here. What the hell took you so long?" Williamson asked. Lopez, for his part, didn't even budge from his spot under the palms.

"Didn't even get to my dessert, you impatient little dickhead," said Nichols.

Then Nichols spotted the dead body and nothing else mattered. "What have we here?" He bent over the body, his hands tucked into his pockets. He made clicking sounds with his tongue every few seconds, his face aglow in delight.

Stella decided that Lopez was right. The man was creepy.

Jody Nichols conducted his initial appraisal of the lifeless body in less than ten minutes. After the deceased was loaded into an ambulance and on his way to the morgue, the pair of cops followed a walkway around the other side of the house to the front door. Stella ran up the backyard deck stairs to the screen door and slid back inside just in time to hear Nikki yell from the kitchen. "Door's open!"

The cops came in quietly, respectfully. Williamson observed Stella for a long moment and she knew what he was thinking: he was expecting a sobbing, emotional wife. Stella was neither.

"Ma'am, my name is Tom Williamson. I just wanna say how sorry I am. I know this is very hard, but we're going to have to ask you and your boy to leave the premises until the investigation over."

"Why?"

"It's an active crime scene, ma'am", Williamson said. "We can't risk contamination of evidence."

Stella sighed. "Is that really necessary?"

"I'm afraid so," he said. "We need to ask you some questions, but first we need to clear the house. Is there somewhere you can stay for a few days?"

"I got you, Stell," Nikki chimed in. "You can stay at Hotel Nikki. I've got a pull-out sofa with your name written all over it!"

Stella shook her head. "We're not leaving."

"Mrs. Callahan," began Lopez, "I understand that

you want to stay here, but we can't allow that. Until forensics clears it, the house and yard are a crime scene. No one, including you and your son, are allowed in that crime scene. If we're figure out what killed your husband, ma'am, we need to do a thorough and complete search for evidence."

Stella slumped into a chair, tired and irritated. It wasn't bad enough that he drank himself to death, now Louis was getting them kicked out of their house too. If he was still alive, she'd have plenty to say to him.

"You'll have to arrest me, then, 'cuz I'm not leaving."

Lopez and Williamson exchanged a look and then stepped into the kitchen to confer. After only a few moments, Williamson joined Stella on the sofa. Lopez motioned for Nikki to follow him out to the screened-in porch.

"I have some questions for you, Mrs. Callahan, and it's important for you to tell me as much as you can."

Stella nodded, but didn't speak.

"Tell me everything that happened today, from the time you woke up."

"All right, well. Here you go. I went fishing while Louis and Matt were still asleep. When I came back, Louis was dead." Stella looked away.

Williamson pulled a pen and a tattered notepad from his front pocket. "What time did you leave the house, ma'am?"

"I don't know. Eight-thirty or nine. Probably closer to eight-thirty."

"Did you see anyone? Talk to anyone?"

"No."

"What about the stitches on his head?" asked

Williamson. "They looked pretty fresh."

"He got those last night." Stella knew that Williamson knew about the concussion and was playing dumb to see what she'd say. "He was driving drunk. When we got home from the emergency room, he promised to stop drinking. He promised! I wanted to believe him."

"Mrs. Callahan, did your husband have any enemies? Any illegal activity that he was somehow connected to?"

"I'm sure you know he was an ex-cop, and that he retired years ago. He didn't need enemies; he was his own worst enemy. He got a concussion. They told him if he drank he could die. He drank. He died."

"So, there's nothing more you know? No private investigation work he was involved with?"

Stella felt surprise wash over her face. Then incredulity. She laughed bitterly. "If he was still working, and I mean doing anything of value to this world, you could have fooled me."

"And what about your son?"

"What about my son?"

"Is he here? Can we speak to him?"

They were interrupted by a racket erupting from the porch. Nikki came pounding into the room. "I'm Stella's best friend and, I swear on my life, she had every right to kill him. He was a very difficult man to live with."

Lopez followed Nikki into the living room wearily. Williamson looked up at Nikki then back at Stella.

"Had you and your husband been fighting, Mrs. Callahan? Any problems in the marriage?"

Stella laughed bitterly. "Of course. Louis was a

goddamn drunk and … have you ever lived with an alcoholic?" Well, let's just say it's not pleasant." Stella grabbed a throw pillow and hugged it to her chest. "But no, I didn't kill him. I actually thought we might have a pretty decent future ahead of us after last night."

"What exactly happened last night?" Williamson asked.

A sound from outside made Stella stand up again, bite her lip, and look out the window at the canal. She knew that sound and it made her stomach turn. It was the hum of a yuppie Bayliner pulling up to her dock.

With lightning speed, Stella was through the kitchen and onto the porch. She threw open the screen door, raced down the steps, and tore right through crime scene tape, waving her arms and screaming, "Get the hell away from my yard, you nosy bastard! You've got no right to be here!"

"That's where you're wrong, Stella!" Her nemesis, in his full Grody gear with pressed dress shorts and collared shirt, waved a finger at her. "I knew you were lobstering this morning, and on a hunch I thought I'd come by to check. And sure enough, from where I'm standing, I can see some evidence of illegal catch on board that death trap."

Williamson and Lopez both jogged down to the dock behind her.

Grody was about to throw his leg over the side of his boat and stride triumphantly over the crime scene tape to Stella's boat when Lopez stopped him.

"Sir," said Lopez, jogging up, badge made even shinier by the falling rain, "This is a possible crime scene. Stay off the dock."

Grody obliged, but reluctantly. "Well, officer, I am

glad the law finally caught up to this woman."

Lopez looked at Stella. She looked back, helpless, her fists and teeth clenched.

Lopez leaned in close to her and whispered. "Is there anything you want to tell me?"

She shook her head, still glaring at her neighbor in the canal.

"Lopez, I'll radio dispatch to send Fish and Wildlife over," Williamson said. His partner nodded.

Lopez approached the small fishing boat at the end of the dock and Stella watched him visibly flinch as he caught a whiff of something dead. She knew the stink couldn't be blamed on Louis, he was well on his way to the meat locker. Stella stood in mute fury, sending daggers into Grody who stood near the gunwale, cleaning his fingernails, careful to keep his perfectly styled hair under his boat's Bimini top and out of the rain.

Fifteen minutes later, an FWC boat approached the Callahan's dock. Lopez stepped into Stella's boat and helped the officer tie up against it. They spoke too quietly for anyone else to hear.

Grody could no longer contain himself. "I think you'll find the bait well full of illegals. Name is Dave Grody, by the way. I've been watching this one for a while. I knew she was lobstering, but I just couldn't catch her. Looks like my luck has changed!" Grody shifted his weight from one foot to the other and back, anxious to see what the bait well held.

"Do you have to look so happy about it? The woman just lost her husband." Lopez shook his head.

Grody stopped rocking. For a second, he looked almost sheepish, glancing around at the officers and

Stella's red eyes as if he hadn't seen them before. "Sorry to hear that. Just doing my job."

The FWC officer stepped into Stella's boat. "What a dick," he muttered. Lopez nodded. He watched over the other officer's shoulder as he opened the holding tank behind the center console.

"Aw fuck," Lopez said.

Stella knew Lopez saw that she had at least fifteen medium-sized lobsters in her possession and they'd been there long enough to stink.

"Williamson," he hollered, "we've got a problem! Gimme a hand, will you?"

"Bingo!" Dave Grody slapped a manicured hand on this thigh. "I knew it! How many does she have, Officer? Are we looking at jail time?"

"You've done your job, Mr. Grody. We'll take it from here."

Grody ignored the officer's attempt to dismiss him. "I always have time to see justice served."

"Oh, go to hell, you pathetic little excuse for a man." Stella, eyes bright with fury, ran toward Grody's boat with the full force of her slender body, but Williamson caught her and held her back.

"Stay the hell on your boat and shut up," Williamson barked to Grody. "Before I have you arrested for interfering with an investigation."

"And disturbing the peace!" Stella chimed.

Grody's face went pale. He was watching Williamson with small, squinting eyes. Grody'd thrilled at the idea of putting others in jail, but when the tables were turned he looked about ready to wet his pressed short pants. He stood at the center console, scratching his balls with both hands, a hilarious quirk Stella had seen only a couple of times before when Grody'd been dealing with particularly intimidating and angry law breakers. She felt a tiny little bit better, and she almost wished he'd get off the boat so she could finish him off. There were a lot of things she'd wanted to say to Louis that she could happily scream at Grody instead.

But that satisfying image faded quickly. The FWC officer was rummaging through her skiff and she was going to be handed her ass one way or another. In the distance she was vaguely aware of the noise of boats running up and down Snake Creek. The stink of rotting lobsters wafted by, making her already sour stomach cramp with nervous anxiety. She knew she was screwed, she just didn't know how badly. *Fuck me. As if a dead husband wasn't enough.*

"Excuse me, Mrs. Callahan." She turned to find Lopez standing next to her. He smiled. "I'd like to have a word alone with you."

Stella followed the officer to small bed of spiny bromeliads, away from the others. The rain felt good on her skin. He leaned in and spoke quietly. "Is it possible that your husband pulled those lobsters without your knowledge? Maybe while you were still asleep?"

Stella shook her head. "No. I did it. Grody knows I did it."

Lopez took a step closer. "You're in shock and you're not thinking straight. You knew nothing about those lobsters. Louis must have taken them this morning before you got up. Isn't that right?"

Stella suddenly got it. "Yeah. Now that you mention it, I think you're right. I didn't even know they were there."

"It's okay, Mrs. Callahan." Lopez put his mostly

useless left hand on her shoulder. "You stay here. I'll put this mess to bed. No worries."

"Hey, Stella!" a Long Island accent bellowed from the back porch and nearly across the canal, "How long has this chili been in the fridge? I'm starving!"

"Too long, Nikki. Like a week and a half. Don't eat it. Why don't you go pick up some groceries?"

"All right! But you're payin!"

"There's some cash in the jar. Now get the hell out of here, Nikki!"

"All right, but I'm also getting beer. You don't need to teetotal anymore."

Stella sighed, wondering about the ironies of life: the kindness of strangers, the uselessness of friends. In her experience, people weren't helpful unless they wanted something in return. She wondered what in the hell Lopez thought she had to give. Williamson closed the bait well. He and the FWC officer stepped onto the dock and Lopez joined them. The trio conferred quietly with their backs to Grody. Their obvious slighting of his authority brought out the aggressor in him. He was impatient for justice to be hammered out.

"What's the plan, Officers?" Grody shouted from his Bayliner. "Time's a-wasting!"

"Show's over." Lopez smiled as he ambled toward Grody's boat. "Turns out Mr. Callahan pulled those illegal lobsters, and since he's dead, there won't be any arrest made. Thanks for your help, but you can be on your way."

"What?" Grody jumped over his gunwale and nearly met Lopez face-to-face. The Officer had the advantage of height, but Grody didn't back down. "You've gotta be kidding me! You know darn well she took those lobsters! I saw her out there this morning!'"

Lopez put up his hands and shook his head. "Calm down, Mr. Grody. Can you prove Mrs. Callahan did it? Do you have photos?"

Grody stomped his foot. "This is total B.S.!" Stella stifled a giggle as she watched from her vantage point in the side yard. He was turning a beautiful shade of purple.

"You did your job, and we thank you for that. Now please, let us do ours," said Williamson. "Why don't you be on your way, sir?"

Grody's color deepened and he turned an eagle eye on Stella, particularly her hands. "Look! She's all scraped up. Those are fresh wounds! Proof she was picking at spiny lobsters all morning. Getting stung like she deserves."

Stella held up her hands and turned then back and forth innocently. "No, Mr. Grody. These are from working in the bromeliad beds. Those bastards are sharp!"

"Just wait until the sheriff hears about this!" Grody scratched his undercarriage with one hand while he pointed at the officers with the other. "You make me sick! Cops like you should be behind bars!"

Williamson wrinkled his brow. "I don't enjoy repeating myself, sir. Be on your way."

Ball sack firmly in hand, Dave Grody boarded his boat, muttering about what he'd tell the sheriff. In spite of the canal's no-wake zone, he sped off. Stella smiled when she saw that even as he rounded into Snake Creek, he was still scratching.

The cops and Stella made their way back to the

house as the forensic team arrived and began their work. Halfway to the stairs, Stella paused, turned to Lopez. He had nice symmetrical features and looked youngish, probably late thirties at most. He reminded her of that handsome cop played by Jimmy Smits on NYDP Blue. He'd saved her ass for no reason other than he felt sorry for her. Or maybe it was a cop trick, trying to get her to trust him so she'd spill her secrets. Well, she had no secrets. If she'd wanted to kill Louis, she'd have done it years ago. She took a moment to look him straight in the eye and say thanks for what he did. He nodded and gave her the slightest of winks.

Then he and Williamson spoke quietly for a minute. When they were done, Lopez left them to speak the officers combing the yard for evidence.

Williamson and Stella went back into the house.

"We'll have to take your full statement again.," Williamson said. "The police records are going to contradict the FWC record. That's going to be a problem. But we need the real story here, this is the serious stuff."

"Why are you helping Lopez cover up for me?" Stella asked. She was too tired and overwhelmed for any more bullshit.

Williamson paused. "Because I think this is an open and shut case and I'd like to get it done without any complications."

Stella nodded. Fair enough.

"But for now," the officer opened his notepad, "you've stated that you woke up around 7 a.m. this morning. You spent an hour plus searching for and dumping all the alcohol you could find in the house. Louis was asleep in bed when you left at approximately

8:30. He was sleeping off a hangover, plus he'd been to the hospital late last night and diagnosed with a concussion."

"That's what happened. What I can't figure out is where he got that bottle of gin. I'd thrown everything out. Everything." Stella's voice was smaller now. The fight with Grody, the search, the relief at her narrow escape had knocked the wind out of her.

"Where's Hammond?" she suddenly asked, almost childlike. "Officer Hammond was one of Louis' best friends."

"Hammond doesn't work this particular beat," Williamson said, and Stella knew he was being diplomatic. She liked Chris Hammond but figured you only get called out to something like this, a somewhat suspicious death, when you've earned it. And as far as she could tell, Chris hadn't earned his way onto anything more than a buy-ten-get-one free card at Dairy Queen.

"Your son was here, asleep as well, when you left?"

"Yes."

"Can you be sure? Did you see him in his bed?"

"Why would you ask me that?" Stella felt, through a fog of exhaustion, her hackles starting to raise again.

"You tell me. Teenage boys do all sorts of things that keep them out all night."

"Not my son."

"Is he an early riser?"

Stella laughed a dry laugh. "Not hardly."

"I'll need to take his statement."

"I'm coming with you."

"Ma'am, he's eighteen, which means he's an adult and can give his own statement. What I'd like you to do right now is just let me do my job."

Stella walked down the hall and knocked on Matt's door. He didn't answer. "Matt? Could you come out? Officer Williamson has a few questions."

Still no answer. She knocked again and then turned the knob, which she handled with care since it was missing a screw and hung at an angle. Stella looked into Matt's bedroom, cramped with piles of dirty clothes and sports gear. The window facing the street was open. Faded, blue curtains gently rustled in the light breeze.

"Goddammit!" hissed Williamson behind her.

PATTYCAKES

Pattycakes Farley googled The Snatch Patch and got a phone number. She spoke to a breathy woman who told her to stop in after six and ask for Sam. It was as she'd hoped: they needed female bartenders.

Patty was just shy of thirty, which by Islamorada standards was quite young, but by sexy bartender standards was basically geriatric. She knew her age wasn't in her favor, so she'd have to look deliciously young and sexy if she stood a chance of being hired. Having worked only menial jobs, Patty's wardrobe wasn't exactly provocative. She made her way back to the Lorelei, found her duffel bag, which had stayed mostly dry, and pulled out her sluttiest outfit: a denim mini skirt and an off-the-shoulder billowy blouse. As she changed in the Lorelei bathroom, Patty remembered how much she hated the blouse because it looked like something a pilgrim might have worn. On the plus side, it would be easy to yank up in case she had to show 'the girls'.

The Lorelei bathroom didn't even have a mirror. Where there should have been one hanging above the bathroom sink was instead a tattered poster of the crew from the Love Boat. Fucking Florida. But she loved it anyway.

Patty hopped her way out the door as she pulled

on first one mule and then its mate, once again glad she wasn't just relegated to the crappy sandals she'd been wearing, and happy to be hiding her gnarly toes.

Fifteen minutes later, the neon sign of The Snatch Patch appeared like an oasis. Patty was surprised by the location. She'd imagined the strip club would be hidden behind a warehouse or alone on a dead-end street. Not in Islamorada! The Snatch Patch was in the midst of restaurants, art galleries, and a bookstore looking like it had every right to be there.

The walk had made her overheated, in spite of the falling rain, and as she approached the parking lot, Patty wiped sweaty palms on the hem of her damp skirt. It wasn't her first visit to a strip club but it was her first time going to one to ask for a job. The blacked-out windows offered no encouragement. She yanked open the heavy door and came face-to-face with a large, fat man.

"Oh, hey." Patty felt her cheeks flush. "Whassup?"

He gestured up the stairs.

"Um, I'm here to apply for a bartending job." Patty tried to sound confident despite the quiver in her voice.

"Bartender, huh? You know that means you show your titties, right? You up for that, sweetheart?" The man's neck looked like a tree stump.

She stuck out her chest. "Yeah, what's the big deal?"

"Well, then, let's see whatcha got. Show me them titties, girl!"

"Just tell me where the manager is."

The bartender shook his head and laughed. "Maybe you should toss back a few shots before you talk to him, honey. You gotta be able to whip those things out if you wanna work here."

Patty laughed nervously. "No worries, they call me the Titty Whipper back home!" She hustled up the red-carpeted steps, anxious to be away from the bouncer before he saw through her fake bravado. He'd been right though. She was in dangerous proximity to sober.

At the top of the staircase, a long bar hugged the left wall of the club and two or three small stages were scattered across the room. Patty avoided looking at the naked girl on the pole and headed straight for the bar. It was dinner time on a Monday but girls were dancing and men were drinking. She sat with her back to the nakedness, but watched with great interest at the skin being reflected in the mirror behind the bar. Patty was envious of the dancer's agility and decided she was most certainly fuckable. That chick has some big balls, she thought, but if I had a body like that, I'd do it too.

"Whataya drinking?" The young bartender turned to her. The woman had small breasts, a slender waist, and a very pretty, feline face. She appeared comfortable talking to a stranger while her small tits sat there for anyone to see.

"How 'bout a Miller Lite and a shot of tequila." Patty grabbed a bar napkin and wiped her brow. "It's hot in here."

"Not as hot as it is outside. Besides, it makes people drink more."

A large balding man sat three stools down. Patty figured he was in his mid-fifties and based on his sweaty and swollen meaty body, she decided he was most certainly not fuckable. He didn't seem interested in the half-naked bartender behind him. He was focused on the naked girl grinding away against the pole.

After ordering another beer and a second shot, she mustered the courage to ask a question. "Where can I find the manager? I'm here for a bartending job."

The topless girl's eyes went straight to Patty's chest. "We do need help. Lemme see if he's free. Hang on." After a quick whisper on her cell, she pointed to a door in the back. "Go on in, he's waiting."

Patty pried herself off the barstool and aimed for the office door. She was rewarded with a close-up of the dancer's asshole. *What the hell am I doing? Daddy would roll over in his grave if he knew what I was up to.*

The door was painted black and looked like it once hung in a prison or mental hospital. It took all of Patty's strength to force it open and it almost closed before she could squeeze through. One meager bulb hung from an exposed electrical socket overhead. It provided enough light to paint the hall in a way that reminded Patty of a horror movie. The dull beat of the music barely penetrated the concrete walls. There was no other sound.

"Hello?" She sounded like every dumb movie broad right before they get whacked from behind in the boiler room. "Anybody here?"

The sound of a chair scraping on a tile floor further down the hall broke the silence. A man popped his head around the doorframe and waved. "Yo!" He disappeared back into the room. Images from movies like Hostel faded from her overactive imagination. Patty headed toward the door.

She knew she had to look sexy if she stood any chance of being hired. She tried to slink down the hall in a provocative way, but tripped and fell to the dirty floor. She stood, brushed herself off, and resumed her normal, rather butch way of walking. "Hi. I'm Patty. They call me

Pattycakes." She reached out her hand to a man behind a desk.

He didn't look up. "Whattya want, Pattycakes?" He dug through a pile of paperwork. Just like the asshole at the Lorelei.

"Um, well, I'm looking for a bartending job."

"Yeah, I figured you wasn't here to dance." He kept his eyes glued to the papers on the desk.

Patty wasn't exactly sure how to take the remark, but it didn't sound like a compliment. "I heard you're hiring?"

"Depends." The man finally glanced up. He had fierce dark eyes, and was attractive in a demonic sort of way.

"Okay . . . on what?"

"You local?"

Patty had learned her lesson. "Yeah."

"How long you been there?"

"A few months."

"Where you been workin' 'til now?"

"I wasn't working. I was…writing. Writing a book, but I ran out of money and need a job." Patty didn't know where that came from. She'd never had an ounce of interest in writing a book. But she'd seen a made-for-TV movie about a writer who lived in a little rented house by a beach in the Florida Keys and solved crimes in her spare time. Seemed like a good life. Hey, beats working.

"A writer, huh? Whattya write? Cheesy romance novels or kinky sex books? Never mind, I don't care. Ain't much of a reader, myself. You have family down here? People?"

"No, just me."

"You famous? Got any books out there?"

"Nope." Patty went red. "Just trying to get that first one done."

"Let's see your tits."

Patty's knees almost buckled. "Wait. What? Don't we talk first? I mean I'm not afraid to show my tits. I do it all the time. Walk around with them hanging out so often at home that the neighbors don't give me a second look. Well, I mean, they look. Of course they look, because these tits are nice." She pointed both thumbs at her chest. "They're really nice. But they're so used seeing them, that…"

"You aren't cut out for this, lady. Go find a job at the library." He went back to his paperwork.

Patty turned and walked out, kicking herself for being such a prude. Before she could talk herself out of it, she ripped off her top and walked back in. She twisted both nipples while rocking her hips. She had the man's attention. Dropping her mini skirt to the floor, she turned her backside to the stranger. Patty did her best to mimic the stripper's move that had given everyone a view of her under carriage. For good measure, she tried to clap her butt checks together in rhythm with the music pounding on the other side of the wall.

"Easy there, hun," he said. "This ain't no proctology visit. You'll do just fine. Go back out and talk to Carla. She'll give you a schedule and answer any questions. Oh, and you're gonna wanna lose ten pounds and trim that beaver if you plan on takin' any dancin' shifts. That thing looks like Orphan Annie on a bad hair day."

"Yeah, I don't plan on dancing, but thanks. I'll keep

that in mind … unless …" Patty said, suddenly nervous. "Any way I can make three hundred by Wednesday, do you think?"

"Like I said, you're in no shape to dance. Bartenders do okay here, but you won't make that kind of money right off the bat. Why you need it?"

"Gotta get my car fixed."

"Well." Sam's voice lifted thoughtfully, like something was just dawning on him. "A newbie can only make that kind of money during private events. You're a lucky girl. We have a special event going on tomorrow night. You go down, talk to Carla, work tonight, tomorrow afternoon, and then the event tomorrow night, and I guarantee you'll make that money. "

"A special event?"

"Yeah. Closed. You know. Private."

"Okay, yeah. I can do that."

This was too good to be true. Patty was ready to work her ass off for the next day and half, get her money, and get the hell out before the storm hit. She'd be spending the night on the beach, though, and she was going to look like shit tomorrow, she already knew. She hadn't wanted to press her luck and ask for a place to stay, too. They were probably reserved for the really committed, long-term staff, but she was desperate.

"Also, I hear you might have a place to stay? For staff?"

"Of course. We have rooms for all our girls. But you already got a place, right?" Sam's voice was smooth, his look wide-eyed and innocent.

"Just . . . It's just that it's not as fortified as this place. I'm getting a little worried. Because of the storm."

"Yeah, we'll set you up. Carla will get you situated—

if your shift works out. Don't fuck up."

"Thanks so much. So, what's your name? Or should I just call you Boss?"

"Sam. But Boss is good too."

Patty's first shift was easy. She bar-backed most of the night, poured a few drinks at the end of her shift, and when it was over, Carla showed her to a small room in the barracks- like building attached to The Snatch Patch.

The room was small and dank and strangely cold, even with the blanket on the bed. Patty kept herself warm by letting herself drift in to nicer thoughts, like being slapped into handcuffs while a certain police officer had his way with her. And she drifted off to sleep having, in some part of herself, already made up her mind to fuck him before she left.

DAY TWO

$STELLA$

In her modest house on one of the canals off Snake Creek, Stella was alone in bed. It wasn't the first time. Louis was usually too drunk to walk further than the living room sofa, where he'd collapse and pass out for the night. She'd always hoped that someday he'd prove stronger than the gin, but Louis didn't live long enough to win that battle. Stella tossed and turned, ticking off all of the things that Louis had mostly taken care of. With plenty of reminders and good old-fashioned hen pecking, he'd dealt with the hurricane, flood, and car insurance policies. He mostly paid the bills and kept the boat running so that Stella could keep food on the table. She was aggravated by the long list of additional responsibilities she'd have to take on, but at least she wouldn't have to deal with a goddamn drunk.

She had never stayed in bed so late into the day. Stella wearily pulled on an oversized t-shirt and tiptoed to the kitchen. The clock on the microwave read 1:09 pm. Already afternoon and she still had so much to do. She absentmindedly opened the fridge, grateful that Nikki had the foresight yesterday to leave a few beers and some pre-made potato salad. She felt a moment of appreciation for Nikki and then pushed it away. Nikki was too much work, and Stella was tired of dealing with other people's bullshit.

On her way to the screened-in porch, she tossed the beer cap into the sink. Stella wondered for the hundredth time how Louis had stashed a bottle of gin without her finding it, and a brand he never drank. Unless he hadn't stashed it. Unless someone had come by.

For an early morning drink?

She frowned at the fleeting thought that while she'd been out lobstering, someone might have come by to offer Louis a lethal dose of hair of the dog. Of course, if somebody had just stopped in for a drink, he or she wouldn't have meant to kill Louis. How could anyone have known that Louis had a concussion? She paused, considered the alternative: that if someone had known about Louis' concussion, and had wanted to hurt him, they'd provided the perfect weapon. But that was crazy. She'd told the truth to the police—Louis wasn't the kind of man who had enemies. Besides, no one had known about his concussion. She dismissed the idea. Williamson didn't think there was any foul play. Murders didn't happen in Islamorada. It wasn't a high-crime island. It was a tiny and quiet, family-oriented village. People moved there to get away from violence and noise, or to finish out their retirements in peace.

If Williamson didn't think there was any foul play, then why did she keep replaying Lopez' words? *So you don't know anyone who'd want to harm him?*

She got on the horn and called Lopez, who said that he and Williamson were on their way over to get Matt's statement. Of course. She looked down at her sagging breasts under the baggy shirt and decided that a bra was a necessary accessory when cops are involved. With more than a little resentment, she changed her outfit and then called to Matt, who was hiding in a sleepy haze.

Her son had disappeared at the absolute worst time the night before. It had thrown Stella for a loop, but Matt had later texted to explain that he'd gone for a bike ride and ended up at Coach's house. Stella was angry but relieved, and told him as much, but she figured he needed space to process his dad's death. She'd told Williamson and Lopez to come back the next day for Matt's statement.

Stella opened the front door for the officers when they arrived. She waved them in from the pouring rain and motioned for them to follow her upstairs.

Matt was sitting in a leather recliner in the living room, drinking a Coke. "Hey, Matt," said Williamson. "Glad to see you're home again. Gave your mother quite a scare."

Matt shrugged and took a sip of soda. Then banged a closed fist against his chest and produced a loud, wet belch.

Lopez cleared his throat. "Now that you're here, we need to ask you a few questions. Please be as honest as you can and tell us everything you can remember, okay?" He put his hand on the boy's shoulder and gave it a small squeeze. "We're both very sorry about your dad, Matt."

The officers sprawled out, trying to make Matt more comfortable by appearing casual. Stella once read that witnesses are more likely to talk if the person asking the questions acts like an interested friend. It was true: most people love to talk about themselves. She hated the idea that her son was being manipulated, but at least they allowed her to stay this time. She guessed they were following some other leads, or maybe by now realized that separating mother and son wouldn't get them anywhere.

"Matt, where were you between seven and ten yesterday morning?"

Matt stared at his soda can. "Asleep."

"Where were you sleeping?" asked Williamson.

"In bed."

Williamson folded his hands in his lap. "In bed where?"

"Here." Matt met Williamson's gaze. "At home."

"And where were you from ten to two-thirty?"

"At practice. I'm assistant coach for the junior football team. We practice at the high school."

Stella felt her temper rise. The questions were aggravating because they were aimed at her baby, who was obviously innocent. To keep her hands busy, she grabbed a stack of mail from the coffee table and pretended to be interested in it. She clicked her tongue periodically, pretending to be annoyed by overdue notices, but it was the conversation around her that caused the irritation.

"Did you hear anything out of the ordinary?" asked Lopez.

Matt shook his head.

"Do you know anyone who would have wanted to kill your father? Anyone who might have wanted him dead?"

"You mean other than me and Mom?"

"Matthew Callahan!" Stella dropped the latest bill and covered her mouth with both hands. "What a terrible thing to say!"

Matt crushed the empty can and tossed it onto

the dusty coffee table. "Don't pretend we were a happy family, Mom, 'cuz everyone knows we weren't." He crossed his arms over his chest and scowled at his lap.

Stella was on her feet. "Just because something's true doesn't mean it has to be shared with the whole damn world!"

Matt laughed bitterly. "Really, Mom? I heard you say it yesterday!" He shrugged. "Who cares anyway? He sure didn't."

Williamson leaned in, making strong eye contact with Matt. "Son," he said, "please answer the question."

"No, I can't think of anyone who would have wanted him dead. He wasn't really like that. He wasn't mean, he was just a drunk."

"Do you think your mother could have killed your father?"

Stella gasped. Matt looked at her for a few moments and then shook his head. "Step-father. And no way. You got that? No. Way."

Stella glared at Williamson. "It's Tom, isn't it?"

Williamson nodded.

"Well, Tom, haven't we been through enough without this crap?"

"We're sorry, Ma'am, but it's a question we had to ask," Lopez said. "Matt, why did you leave the house the day your father died? Where did you go?"

Stella answered first. "He just needed to get away."

Williamson looked at Stella and tried to deliver a friendly smile. It was more like a grimace. "Ma'am, please let your son answer. It's important we get *his* statement." Matt stared at his lap, tears collecting in the corners of his eyes. "Where did you go, Matt?"

"To Coach's house."

"Matt, did you kill your father?" Lopez said.

Stella kicked the leg of the coffee table, sending the empty soda can over the edge and onto the floor. "That's enough!"

Lopez stood and rested his hands on Stella's shoulders, which heaved up and down as she sucked in big gulps of air. "Mrs. Callahan, we aren't trying to upset you, but these are questions we have to ask."

"Of course I didn't kill him!" Matt said.

Stella pushed his hands from her shoulders. "What the hell is wrong with you people?" She turned her back to the officers and covered her mouth with one hand. "I think you should go." Her voice cracked.

"We're just trying to rule all out possibilities here," Williamson said. "It will help us catch our guy faster."

"I didn't kill him," Matt whispered. "I didn't."

Stella turned and looked lovingly at her only child. "I know, honey. Everybody knows that."

Williamson waited a second or two before standing. "If either of you think of anything else, please call us right away," he said.

Stella followed them to their vehicle parked on the road and reached a hand toward Lopez. "Hey, do you think it's possible someone came here and killed Louis? Like maybe they provided him with booze knowing it would do him in?"

Williamson reached to his duty belt and turned down the volume of the radio clipped to his side. Dispatch's instructions were temporarily silenced. "Mrs. Callahan, we all know that your husband had a concussion and shouldn't have been drinking, but I doubt if there's a rogue band of criminals making their way through the Keys looking for people suffering from concussions so that they can pass out liquor as a means to murder. It's just not logical."

Williamson stepped into the driver's seat and tilted his head out the window. "It's an open and shut case."

Lopez scanned the outside of the house. "Ma'am, you and Matt better take the rest of the day and get this place boarded up. After that, the safest thing for you to do is pack a bag and spend a few days with family or friends on the mainland. Better yet, get up to Alabama or Georgia, out of the way of the storm completely."

Stella sighed. "We don't have any family." She looked at the house and sighed. "I can't think of anywhere to go and I think we'd both rather be here, in our own home, than at someone else's anyway."

"We can't force you to leave," Lopez said, "but Ma'am—Stella—I'm telling you this is not the safest place for you right now."

"Maybe Hammond can come and help us. He was Louis' closest friend."

Lopez's eyebrows reached for the sky. "Really?" He glanced briefly at Williamson before returning his gaze to Stella. "Thanks for letting us know. Get a motel in Mobile, Mrs. Callahan. Do it for Matt."

"We can't afford it. We're staying put."

Lopez and Williamson left and Stella wearily walked back into the house.

After a brief hug, Matt said, "Mom, you look tired. Like, really tired. I'll go to the store and get some stuff. More bottled water, right? Some canned tuna?"

Stella offered a weak smile at her son. She hated letting him take on her chores, but it was good for him to pick up some slack around the house and stay busy. "And go to Ace Hardware for some boards. Just tell them what you're looking for, they'll know. There's cash in my purse, take it all. Should be enough to cover it. And get extra candles and batteries."

Matt left the living room in a flash and disappeared. Stella rested the beer on a stack of last week's lottery tickets. For years, Stella had set aside as much money as she could to play the weekly lotto. It gave her something to hope for. Maybe one day her ship would come in, but knowing her luck, it'd probably be an inflatable dinghy with a hole in it.

She sipped the beer and again wondered about their safety. She dialed Hammond. He'd need to know about Louis anyway. No answer. She left a message and crawled back in to bed.

The hardest part of her life had just begun and she didn't feel ready.

Stella tried to nap while Matt was out buying provisions, but sleep wouldn't come. Guilt about sending her son out alone into the madness that precedes every hurricane coupled with anger at Louis for being such a shitty husband kept her awake. The house was eerily quiet, except for the ancient air conditioner, which sounded like it was nearly ready to call it quits.

"Stella, girl, you here?"

It was Nikki. Stella wanted to pretend she wasn't home, but it was pointless. Nikki would just let herself in if she didn't answer.

"Come on in, Nikki." Stella checked the time on her cell. Nikki had a habit of showing up at meal time. She reluctantly peeled herself from the bed.

"Hey, girl! Wassup? How's my favorite widow?" She blew kisses as she strutted into the kitchen on a pair of orange stilettos.

"Look at those shoes!" Stella suppressed a grin.

"You can't have them, so don't ask!" Nikki said. "I brought wine and cheese. Thought you might need some company. Patty is about to hit. I like that name. Patty."

"Not me," said Stella. "Reminds me of Peppermint Patty. I always hated Peppermint Patty. So full of herself, calling poor Charlie Brown 'Chuck.' Ugh." Stella saw a slew of bags around Nikki's feet.

"You moving in?"

"Like I said yesterday, might be fun if we're holed up here."

"It was sweet of you to drop by, Nikki, but—" Stella wasn't in the mood for conversation or being holed up anywhere with Nikki.

"No buts! We're gonna have girlfriend time and you're gonna love it!"

Stella rolled her eyes. Getting rid of Nikki was about as easy as getting rid of the clap. She knew she was in for a long night when she spotted the box of shitty white zin that Nikki held like a prize pig at the state fair.

"I hear that's an excellent year."

Nikki scratched her scalp with inch-long acrylic nails painted neon orange to match her shoes. "Huh?"

"Never mind." Stella pushed herself past Nikki to get some wine glasses. She suddenly felt like getting good and drunk.

Nikki handed her friend a pound loaf of Velveeta. Nothing but the best would do. "How 'bout you cut the cheese while I pour?"

Stella laughed. "Cut the cheese. Get it?"

Nikki stared blankly at her friend. "What?"

"Forget it. I'll get the glasses." Louis would have laughed. He loved fart jokes. While Nikki struggled with the spout, Stella sliced Velveeta on a crab-shaped cutting board that Matt had made in junior high and given to her for Mother's Day. "Wanna sit on the porch?"

Nikki dug in her ear with an orange claw. "I dunno. The mosquitoes were pretty bad in the driveway."

Stella dumped a handful of Ritz onto the cutting board. "It's screened-in, remember?"

Nikki scoffed. "There are holes in those screens the size of golf balls. Don't tell me there aren't mosquitoes out there!"

Stella shrugged. "Yeah, I know, but Louis will fix them. He promised."

"Honey, Louis' fixin' days are over. And the only thing he ever fixed in his life was a cocktail."

Stella's left hand darted out and slapped Nikki across the face. Before she could regain her composure, it launched out and whacked the much larger woman a second time.

"What the fuck?" screeched Nikki. She pressed a hand to her cheek. There was an impressive red hand mark underneath. "What the hell is wrong with you?"

Stella smoothed the hem of her top and folded her hands behind her back to keep them from doing more damage. When she spoke, her voice was calm. Even Stella was surprised by how composed she sounded. "Get out of my house, Nikki. Right now."

"You fucking hit me!"

Stella moved her hands to her hips and glared at Nikki. "You insulted my husband. Get out of my house before I hit you again."

"You're fucking nuts, you know that!" Nikki threw

a hunk of processed cheese on the floor at Stella's feet. "I came over here to be nice and you fucking hit me! I could have you arrested!"

Matt leapt up the stairs and into the kitchen, eyes wide. He dropped some grocery bags on the floor. "What's wrong?"

Nikki spun around and threw her arms in the air, revealing hairy pits. "Your crazy mother just hit me in the face! She's a fucking lunatic!"

"I won't tell you again, Nikki. Get out of my house before I throw you out."

Nikki curled her hand into a fist and started toward Stella. Matt jumped between them with his hands out in front, preventing Nikki from getting closer. "Don't even think about it."

Nikki cackled. "Get out of my way, you spoiled little brat." She shoved Matt's chest with both hands. "Mind your own goddamned business!"

Before she could blink, Matt had Nikki pinned against the refrigerator. Her arms were crossed in front of her chest and the grip he had on her wrists ensured they stayed put. "Here's what's gonna happen. When I let go, you're gonna walk out the front door. Understood?"

Nikki spit in Matt's face.

"Oh geez, Nikki!" shouted Stella. "That's disgusting!"

Matt didn't flinch. "I repeat. I'm going to let go and you're going to leave. Do you understand?"

Nikki puffed out her cheeks and exhaled until all the air was gone. She spoke through gritted teeth. "Fine. But I'm taking my wine!" Matt waited a moment and then backed off, putting himself between the two women. Nikki reached over the counter, snatched the box of wine, and pulled it to her ample chest. She flipped Stella the bird and sashayed to the stairs, picking up her bags all at once. "You're gonna regret this, Stella girl. I was all you two had left. Enjoy your lonely existence."

Stella felt suddenly very tired of everything and everyone. Nikki had been a crappy friend, but she had at least tried to be there for Stella in her own, annoying way. She helped Matt get the groceries put away without much commentary and then found herself in reverie looking out the window over the choppy water. Something in the air—the steady rain or maybe the coming storm—made her feel like she desperately needed to get out of the house. But first there was work to be done.

Mother and son spent the rest of the afternoon boarding up the place, trimming trees, and gathering debris from the yard. When they began their work, they were careful to avoid the police tape around the dock, but after a while, Stella got irritated and ripped through it, gathered it into a ball, and stuffed it in a trash can.

"We don't need this shit anymore," she hissed. "It's an open and shut case."

They were just about to call it quits and get out of the rain when they heard the sound of metal scraping the concrete seawall. They'd forgotten about Stella's skiff tied up at the dock.

"Holy crap, Mom!" Matt yelled over the howling wind. "Look how high the canal is!"

Stella shook her head in disbelief. The water level had risen several inches in just a few hours.

"We gotta get that thing tied down!"

Together they pulled the skiff into the concrete

landing under the porch. It was a problem Louis *had* fixed, so take that, Nikki. A couple years back he'd drilled in helical anchors to the landing and procured good straps with almost no stretch. Matt and Stella synced the boat to the ground.

But something was troubling Stella. Something more than the enormous troubles she already had. An inkling. A feeling like something wasn't quite right. She'd been in this mood when Nikki had come over, and now that she'd kicked Nikki out, it was whining in her ear, whatever this thing was.

She thought maybe it was that they still didn't have enough provisions, in spite of the few canned goods and water that Matt brought home. He'd spent the bulk of her money on supplies to board up the house. Back inside, she changed into dry clothes, quickly made Matt a couple of grilled ham-and-cheese sandwiches and some tater tots, and then fought traffic all the way to Winn-Dixie. She found herself there just a little too late. It was 7:15 p.m. according to her cell and the sign on the door apologized to patrons for closing at 7:00 p.m., along with an announcement that they wouldn't open again until Hurricane Patty had left the neighborhood.

Stella found herself in an unfamiliar situation. She was out at night with the car. Matt was safe at home, fed and watching TV, and the storm wasn't expected to hit until the next day. For the first time in many years, Stella had no husband to return to. She was a single woman again. Not that she felt single and ready to mingle, or anything close to that, but she was her own person again, completely. Her sadness was tinged with something odd and exhilarating.

She drove aimlessly towards Islamorada's art

district, craving conversation and companionship. Crowds were something she normally avoided on her days off: a side-effect of her waitressing job. But tonight, when the Lorelei came into view, Stella almost smiled. Louis used to take her there for happy hour when Matt was still in daycare. For less than twenty bucks, they could have a few beers and split a big burger and fries. It had been years since she'd set foot in the place, but Stella felt reluctantly drawn to it.

She parked near a big, beautiful banyan tree and high-tailed it across the pot-holed, gravel lot to the covered deck. She quickly aimed for a spot at the bar, avoiding eye contact with the loud group of locals riding out the storm. She wanted to remain on the crowd's fringe, enjoying the sense of belonging without having to participate.

"Stella!" She recognized the loud voice. It belonged to Matt's football coach. Tommy and his family had relocated from Chicago a few years earlier. He and Sarah, along with their three rough-and-tumble boys, lived a few doors down.

"Tommy Buck, as I live and breathe!"

He was sitting at the bar alone nursing a beer. Stella leaned in and he gripped her in a one-armed bear hug before plastering a wet, loud kiss on her forehead. "I'm so sorry 'bout Louis," he whispered. "Word just made it to da team today. I been meanin' to call."

Stella clung to Tommy for a moment. "Today? I figured Matt would have told you all about it when he was with you yesterday."

Tommy looked confused. "Yesterday? Nah, I haven't seen Matty since Sunday's practice. I told him to take a couple days before he came back, ya know, cuz of the accident."

"What?"

The bartender came over to ask Stella what she was drinking.

"I'll . . . I'll have a vodka martini. Dry. Two olives," she said, and had to stop her voice from trembling.

She turned to Tommy and looked him dead in the eye. "Matt wasn't with you yesterday? Afternoon to late evening? He wasn't with you?"

"No. I was runnin' drills alone with da junior team all afternoon, then home for dinner. You tellin' me Matty said he was with me?"

Stella tried to look casual. "No, I'm sure it's fine. I must be remembering wrong. Sorry."

Tommy leaned closer. "Well, he was probably a mess yesterday. Maybe will be for a while. Just talk to him, he's a good kid. How you holding up?"

"I'm good, Tommy. I'm good." But Stella's hand shook as she raised her martini to her lips, her mind racing over all the possibilities. Matt lied! To me. To the Police! Why? A girl? Certainly, it could be a girl. Or a friend? Why would he have said he was at Coach's house though? Because Coach was safe and Matt knew that she'd let it go at that.

"Tommy, does Matt ever bring anyone to practice? Like to watch? A girl maybe? He's never brought any home, but I think he was sort of ashamed, you know, of Louis, so he kept them away."

"Nah, I mean, not that I can think of. He's kind of a shy kid, though he gets along fine with da other guys on da team."

"You've never seen anyone hanging around?"

Coach was thoughtful for a moment as he sipped

his beer. "Come to think of it, I did see him chattin' with an older chick one day after practice. Attractive. Dark hair. I figured she was a tutor or something, SAT prep, ya know? This was a couple months back."

"Older?"

"Maybe mid-twenties," he said.

Stella swirled her clear salty drink with her cocktail straw then sucked both olives off it. She was thinking.

She didn't know if it bothered her more that an older woman had been talking to her son, or that no girls his own age had. He was a good kid, healthy, kind, and athletic. What's not to like?

It was true, for a couple difficult years he was caught in the awkward and unpredictable stage between boy and man, frustrated because he was neither. He'd gotten into trouble his freshman year for underage drinking when the cops raided a party. Common enough. But then he'd also been busted for weed sophomore year by the school resource officer. But he seemed to straighten up after that. He was always serious about football and then he just became Football Kid, all about the game, eating healthy, staying in shape. He'd graduated in June and had been accepted to both Golf State Community College in Panama, Florida and George Mason University in Fairfax, Virginia. He was one of the best on the high school team, but Islamorada was a small town, and he was a big fish in a little pond. He had gotten partial scholarships, but not full, and Stella didn't know how they'd afford to send him to either college. It was something Louis had promised to figure out this summer.

Louis had always insisted on handling the banking alone and Stella had said okay because that's how they did it back when Louis was growing up. Husbands managed the money and women stayed out of it. She made her own money working at the Cholesterol Hut, which was all cash, but it didn't amount to much. Over the years, Stella began to question their financial position. The electric had been turned off more than once and Stella had to step in and cover it. Whenever she asked Louis to talk about money—bank accounts, investments, whatever he did in his study—he would just say, "Yeah, yeah, when I have time."

Because she was so much younger when they married, and he was already established, she just went along with things. It never felt comfortable to ask how much money he'd saved or what kinds of investments he had. Louis had taken her and Matt in when they were nearly destitute and provided for them in a way Stella couldn't have done on her own. She was content to let the rest take care of itself. For the duration of their marriage, Louis kept the financial information to himself.

"Want another round?" The bartender spoke over his shoulder as he changed the TV channel at the other end of the bar to appease a group of unhappy geezers.

Stella shook her head, which was already swimming.

"I'm sorry, Tommy," she said. "I don't mean to worry you. I'm sure Matt's fine." Stella offered a weak smile. "I appreciate that you're looking out for him, so please tell me if there's anything I need to know about. How are Nicole and the boys?"

Tommy and Nicole were terrific neighbors. Since they'd moved in, they went out of their way to include the entire street in weekend brunches and holiday parties. They always had something going on. Cars coming and going. Kids fishing and swimming. Boats of all sizes pulling in and out. More than once, Betty from across the canal had come over in their dingy with her yappy little mutt to voice her concerns to Stella.

"Are they druggies?" she had asked. "They've got more cars than anyone I know."

Stella had laughed. "Is that how you can tell someone's a drug dealer? By the number of cars they own?"

"You can laugh, but I'm telling you, something's going on over there. Not like my neighbors, who are nice and quiet and bookish, though I'm pretty sure they're lesbians."

Betty had picked up her three-legged dog and pulled it close, as if to protect it from the drug-pushing Buck family. Miss Annabelle wore a polka dot dress and a bow tied around each ear. Stella hated people who dressed dogs—especially yappy dogs—in doll clothes.

"They've got people in and out, in and out. All day long." She lowered her voice to a whisper. "That's not normal."

"Tommy was pro football. He has pro football money. And they have three kids, Betty. Of course it's normal."

"Well, I'm gonna call the police the next time they play that awful music. It makes Miss Annabelle perfectly miserable." The little hairball sneezed, as if in agreement.

"I've got a better idea, Betty." Stella felt reckless. "How about if you try to find a hobby other than watching the Bucks through your husband's binoculars."

Stella had smiled sweetly and walked away.

The canal naturally partitioned the land into two

halves: one on each side of the canal. Betty's side was indeed quieter because the entire street was inhabited by retirees. Stella's side had mostly families with kids and tons of dogs. The houses to the left were bigger than hers, becoming more and more expensive as they neared Snake Creek, giving residents access to both the ocean and the bay. Stella could never afford one of those places. Not in a million years.

Louis' cottage had been a family home, built in the late 1930s, and inherited. The mortgage was long paid off. It was the waterfront property taxes, combined with hurricane and flood insurance, that fashioned the noose around Stella's neck. But she was still better off than many. At least she didn't have to worry about the landlord jacking the rent each year or being forced to move out because the owner got a purchase offer he couldn't refuse. She knew too many people who lived in fear of both, most of them in trailers.

Trailer parks dotted the small island. Tiny pockets of those living hand-to-mouth, overlooked and ignored by those living in the nearby grandiose and overpriced mansions. All in all, Islamorada was awash with the very wealthy and the very poor, all within a few short miles of each other. And the Callahans had to struggled just to stay in the bottom middle. Now that Louis was dead, Stella guessed she'd continue to just barely get by. She was lucky though, she supposed. At least as a cop's widow, she would continue to get his meager pension. But Matt was just going to have to take out student loans, and Stella was probably going to have to work overtime at the Cholesterol Hut.

The smell of fried food distracted Stella from her thoughts and made her mostly empty stomach rumble.

Tommy noticed and without another word ordered Stella a platter of fries piled with chunky chili and gobs of melted cheese.

"Tommy! You didn't have to do that."

"Put a sock in it," he said. "You've brought 'em to every party we've had, so I know you love 'em. Besides, I gotta eat, too."

Stella smiled. "Okay, we'll share. So, you guys staying?"

"No way. We got da house ready to go, and two of da cars packed up. We're leavin' tonight, 3 a.m. That's why I'm here, so I can stay awake while da others get a little sleep. Gonna switch drivers every few hours and just plow all da way through. Stop just for gas and da john. We'd been planning a trip to da Grand Canyon before school starts, thought we might as well do it now."

"How nice. That sounds really nice," Stella said wistfully.

Tommy got quiet and looked a little puzzled. "You know, I spoke to da coach at George Mason, he's under the impression Matty's going there in the fall. But da kid hasn't said a word to me about where he's goin'. Fall semester starts in a month."

Stella's heart dropped. How could she have let this happen? Tommy was right. It was almost August and they'd said yes to a college for Matt back in the spring without knowing how they would pay for it. Louis had said he'd figure it out. And Matt probably knew that and assumed he wouldn't actually be able to go to college. No wonder he'd been acting out.

"Sorry, Stella," said Coach. "Feels like I'm giving you more than your share of shitty news tonight."

The platter of loaded fries was set with a flourish in front of them, but Stella could hardly see it. Tears welled up in her eyes. Her poor boy. His dad was dead, and now the college he'd worked so hard to get into . . . they'd fucked it up. She wished she'd known more about things: about college and money and deadlines. But that hadn't been her life.

Stella had married her high school sweetheart after graduation. He was the only boy she'd ever kissed. They married six weeks after graduation, and three months later Stella was pregnant. She left her him shortly before Matt was born when he nearly put her in the hospital. He was a kid still, they both were, only nineteen. But he had a mean streak she hadn't seen, the stress of having to grow up too fast had released it. She'd never been hit as a child; at first she didn't know what to make of it. But when the cycle kept continuing—fights, accusations, unrealistic expectations—and he pushed her so hard that she almost lost the baby, well that was it. Stella moved back in with her parents and never spoke to that asshole again. He'd never even tried to contact his son, and Stella had always felt that was a blessing and at the same time the saddest heartbreak of her life.

Out of the corner of her eye, Stella thought she saw the back of Hammond's head, but decided it couldn't be him because the red-haired, trashy looking young woman next to him certainly wasn't Carrie. As the two ducked out of the bar to the parking lot, Stella got up.

"Excuse me a sec, Tommy," she said. "I'll be right back."

Stella followed the pair. Sure enough, it was Hammond. He and the little hussy slunk into the front seat of his car. She knew Hammond was having troubles at home. In fact, if Stella were honest, she'd say his wife was a stone-cold yoga-teaching Nazi bitch. But cheating? She considered Hammond a close friend of the family, and this was the last straw on a pile of bad news, uncovered lies, and deepening grief. Plus, she'd tried calling him a number of times to tell him his best friend had died, and there he was with some floozy, too busy to even pick up the phone.

Stella dashed back to the bar, hugged Tommy goodbye, wished him a safe trip, and made her way home through heavy rain. She would try Hammond's landline. She didn't know it, but Louis would have it somewhere, probably on his cellphone, wherever that was.

$\mathcal{B}ART$

Bart was half-asleep on the sofa wearing only a pair of boxers, trying to fight off the nausea. He'd hung around for some afternoon delight yesterday, and then stayed the night. He was feeling more interested in life than he had in a while, but it'd been two days since he ran out of tweek and he was experiencing some definite withdrawal. Some cramping, sweats, runny nose. Once he'd gone a full week without it and that was bad. He vomited. A lot. Had the shits. Mostly he couldn't fucking think straight and every little thing made him want to kill somebody. That was before a methadone clinic opened up on the island. He didn't like to go there—he preferred his drugs in a recreational environment—but if he couldn't find his own, he'd have to get over there somehow.

He'd need a ride home from Tiny, or to call a cab. He couldn't remember what the hell the plan was. And Tiny could always find heroine, meth, coke, whatever they were in the mood for. But something told him to keep Tiny away from this situation as long as possible. He liked this life. He could run Emma's errands, cook her food, and lift her in and out of her wheelchair to shit or piss in the toilet. In return, he could bang her whenever the mood struck and enjoy all the booze he wanted.

Whatever he figured out, it would have to be soon,

or he'd be cast about in waves of irritability and craving. And that would be hard to hide from Emma in this little trailer.

Emma had been an addict too, but she'd been in the hospital four months and who knows, maybe she was going to try to stay clean this time. She probably still had a lot of hook-ups in the neighborhood, but the place looked downright deserted. No one had even stopped by to say hello since they'd come in.

Emma hollered from the deck into the open door of the trailer. "Hey Bart, you better make a run to Winn-Dixie. I don't like the sky right now, looks like a bad storm."

His benefactor sat in her wheelchair on the deck, tending to dozens of clay pots brimming with herbs, orchids, and bromeliads. She'd spent most of her morning outside, under the trailer awning, fiddling with plants, not minding the drizzle.

"Bart? Did you hear me?"

He groaned. "Yeah, I heard you." He stood and scratched his chest. "What the fuck you doing with those things?"

"Just helping them along. They've been neglected."

"Whattaya want from Winn-Dixie?"

"Grab some meat and beer, and maybe some other stuff like bread and chips. And my prescriptions. They're on a sheet on the bedside table with some money. Take what you need."

Bart smiled smugly. He already knew girls like her kept their money stashed around the house—and the bedside table wasn't the only place. Girls who had their own place in the corner of a trailer park, who took care of themselves, but just barely. They didn't have bank accounts, they had hidey-holes. It was all coming to him. He'd find some extra cash, hook up with a dealer he knew in the area while he was out, come back with groceries, meds, and all the drugs he wanted. He quickly looked in her cigar boxes, between sheets in the bedroom linen closet and, lo and behold, he came up with a crisp hundred-dollar bill from an empty tissue dispenser.

His stomach lurched and he had to sit down. The nausea was getting worse, but he clung to that bill like a lifeline. He knew there would be more like that hidden. Searching Emma's dingy trailer for hidden cash would be like the best Easter Egg hunt ever. He just needed to wait until she was sleep—

"Hurry the fuck up! What are you doing in there, Einstein? I'm starving."

Bart threw on a men's pair of swim trunks, a Sloppy Joe's shirt, and flip-flops, all things left behind by Emma's exes. He walked out under the awning, scratching. "All right. Anything else before I take my leave, Boss Lady?"

Emma looked up from her purple basil, a little concerned. She pointed at the old boombox tucked away on top of a kitchen cabinet. "Yeah, switch on the radio, will ya? I wanna hear what's going on with the weather."

The weather. All of a sudden, Bart heard the Lorelei bartender's voice in his head talking about the hurricane, "*Gonna make landfall in a day or two. Looks like it could be a bad one.*"

Fuck. He'd been in such a fog from the withdrawal. Add in day-drinking plus a whole evening and night of good fucking. And then more fog this morning. He couldn't believe he'd forgotten about the fucking hurricane.

Emma didn't know. Hadn't anyone at the hospital

told her? Apparently not. He was about to tell her, but something sneaky and desperate in him said, "Stop." If she knew, she'd start making plans to evacuate. In fact, it was only a matter of time before she caught on that most of the cars in her trailer park were missing, and then the cops or whoever would come by and tell everyone to evacuate. The roads would be tough to drive too. It was mandatory evacuation for people in low-lying areas and mobile homes, and Emma was both.

But most importantly, if Emma left the trailer, he'd have to leave the trailer. And she'd collect up all that precious money first. He could steal it from her, carry out some sort of minor con. Get her safe somewhere up north and then take off. But Emma knew Tiny, she lived in Islamorada, and she knew who the hell he was. If Bart were to try to dump her and steal her cash, he'd have to leave the Keys for good.

No, he'd need to find a way to bleed her slowly. And keep her away from other people. And that meant he'd have to keep her in this trailer through the coming hurricane.

"Hello, Bart? Anybody home?"

"Right, sorry. Just going over my list. Meat, scripts, beer, other shit. What kind of meat?"

"Anything on the grill would be great."

"They don't call me Thrill Meets Grill for no reason, Crip!"

Emma laughed. "Thrill Meets Grill? You really need to work on your self-esteem."

Bart walked over and pushed down his shorts. "I got your meat right here, ma'am. It's hot and juicy, just the way you like it."

Emma took him into her mouth and while he worked her tits with both hands, she slipped one hand between her legs. It was over quickly.

"All right then," Bart said, pulling his pants back up. "I'll be back in a little while."

When Emma wasn't looking, he pushed the boom box further back where she couldn't see it. The last thing he needed was for her to insist about the radio being on and then hear about the hurricane before he had time to figure out a plan. The combination of stretching and looking and up made his head spin. He grabbed ahold of the counter with both hands as the nausea rose, his throbbing skull felt like it was cracking open. His hands shook and he broke out into a cold sweat. He hadn't felt this bad in a while, but he knew he had to fight it. There was money to be had and Bart suspected there was enough of it to make this shit worthwhile.

"Bart?" Emma asked, with real concern in her voice. "Is something wrong?"

The truth never came easily to Bart. Mostly, he never considered telling it. The truth overcomplicated a lot of things and fucked up the rest. "Nope. Just really fucking hungry. Can't wait to eat."

After a quick review of his shopping list, Bart ducked into Emma's Honda. He had half a mind to just take off into the sunset and leave everything behind while he had a couple hours out of Tiny's grasp. But he had a big fish nearly on the hook here and he didn't want to lose it.

The radio announcer was spitting out emergency information, where to go, what to do. And then, a wave of nausea hit, and his hands could barely hold the steering wheel, they were shaking so hard. The traffic was suddenly fucking unbearable. So much traffic, some of it on the way to the Winn-Dixie, like he was. The rest of it was fancy SUVs high-tailing it out of town, boats in tow. That sight, he had to confess, made him smile. Smug, rich fuckers.

Bart honked at an impatient driver in a brand-new Lexus. The fat man behind the wheel, resembling a swollen tick, got fed up with being in traffic and went off-road. The crazy bastard veered off the blacktop and gunned it onto the walking path that ran parallel to the road. He nearly clipped a lady walking an arthritic black lab.

Where are the fucking cops when you need 'em?

The jackass who tried to beat the system by going off road found himself blocked by a huge backhoe and dump truck. Apparently, the county had decided to temporarily suspend roadwork until the hurricane had passed. Like Bart, the other drivers found great satisfaction seeing the Tick Man's progress slowed to a screeching halt. No one would let him squeeze back onto the road. Bart flipped the driver the bird as he crept past, grateful that karma had worked so quickly.

Nearly thirty minutes later, he arrived at his first destination. It was less than six miles north of Emma's neighborhood, but the gridlock of the Overseas Highway made it feel like ten times that. Inside Winn-Dixie, some nasally sounding broad made an announcement every ten minutes that the store was closing at 7 p.m. and wouldn't reopen until after the hurricane. As Bart tried to concentrate on what he was there to buy, she encouraged shoppers to make their final selections and bring them to the checkout. Through waves of heavy nausea, he fought the impatient, agitated crowd, and picked up Emma's prescriptions. The pharmacist handed Bart a sheet of paper along with the little white paper bag.

After cramming the scripts in the front pocket

of his shorts, Bart picked out three juicy T-bones, two cases of Bud, a case of bottled water, and enough chips and pretzels to feed all of the Little League teams in the Upper Keys. At Bill's Liquor next door, he bought a liter of Jim Beam. He chose the Double Oak instead of the Straight Whiskey. It was twice as much, but hell, Emma had the money. Bart wasn't a fancy guy, and part of him wanted to say hey fucktard, just get two bottles of the cheap stuff, but it had been too long since he'd had a top shelf—or even middle shelf—bottle and he wanted to treat himself. Something about all the people around him in a frenzy, abandoning their homes and fleeing for the hills with the sky raining heavy and purple, well, it sort of felt like the end of the world and he liked it. He liked it a lot. Such an event deserved a thirty-dollar bottle of whisky. And some pretzels and shit.

As he paid for the booze, he thought of the weary-looking islanders stocking up on hurricane supplies. If all went well, he and Emma would ride out the storm in a haze of fucking, eating, and drinking. He didn't know how he'd get through it without more tweek, but he'd have to figure something out. He didn't want to go back to his cousin's, not yet. Not with all that cash waiting to be found.

No, he'd just go back to the trailer. Board it up with whatever he could find lying around. Take what he could without her noticing, then go back to Tiny's when it was all over.

That was when Bart felt the pack of meds in his pocket and suddenly had the urge to open it.

What was inside changed everything.

The lucky bitch was on Percocet. Percocet has Oxy in it. Oxy is famous for relieving withdrawal symptoms—his own to be specific—in the right doses.

Side-effects include confusion, drowsiness, blurred vision. Bart grinned. An overdose of this shit could make Emma pass right out.

He just needed to figure out how much to give her to knock her out without killing her, so he had time alone in the trailer to take stock of the situation. He'd need every fucking dollar in that whole fucking place. Emma would be fine. She was getting unemployment, probably also getting disability. She'd be fine. She wasn't his fucking problem.

This discovery called for a celebration. He made a quick call on his cell. It was going to be expensive, but worth it.

"Sea Breeze," Sam said. "I can't make it, but I'll send one of my guys."

Bart tossed the cell onto the passenger seat and headed for the trailer park.

Every site looked like it was recently occupied by campers and mobile homes that had been rooted out by the stems. There were no kids on bikes zigzagging between rows of vacationers, no old ladies in muumuus sitting in fold-out chairs.

Bart turned down the radio and lowered his window, unaffected by the deluge of rain pelting him. He flicked a butt out onto the pea rock flanking the narrow, paved road. A piercing old-lady's voice rose beyond a window, followed by the lonely baying of a hound dog. "Hey, that's my yard, you moron. Show some respect!"

Bart flipped the bird absentmindedly and drove on. He soon found what he was looking for. The trailer park was oceanside, the kind of place that is still fairly cheap but affords an ocean view. Near the back of the park stood a couple of green dumpsters, partially surrounded by fencing. Parked between the dumpsters and water's edge was a black Range Rover with tinted windows being beaten by the rain. Exchanges like this were best and easiest during a crisis, he'd learned. Cops had bigger fish to fry. Bart pulled alongside as the driver stepped out without too much caution. It wasn't anyone Bart remembered dealing with before and he was a little surprised by how young the kid looked, but Bart's needs far outweighed his curiosity. If the Queen Mother herself handed over the drugs, he wouldn't have been less interested.

"Sam said this is the best he could do on such short notice. He needs everything else for tonight."

"What's tonight?" Bart asked.

"Didn't your cousin tell you?"

"No. Been with a broad for the past day or so."

"Well, if you're coming tonight with your cousin, Sam said there will be plenty of good stuff there." The kid smacked his forehead. "Oh, yeah, he told me to tell you no chicks. Don't bring any chicks."

"Why not?" Bart somehow held back the urge to vomit. Sweat trickled down his hairline and his scalp itched. He eyed the vial in the kid's hands, desperate to get whatever it was pumping through his veins.

"It's a Hurricane Party."

"Ohhhh." Bart had heard about those. Holed up with tons of drugs, liquor, and all the broads you could fuck. But it was usually a big buy-in. A lot more than he had on him for sure.

He had to think. "Hey, do me a favor. Don't tell Tiny you saw me."

"Whatever, I don't give a shit." The kid handed over a little vile and Bart exchanged it for the hundred.

The kid turned to go.

"Hey, what's the buy-in?"

"In your case, I'd say the buy-in is talking to Tiny."

Bart didn't last thirty seconds. He snorted the vile immediately in the front seat of the Honda. Feeling significantly better, and boosted by the Percocet riding shot gun, Bart decided to make an extra effort to keep himself and Emma safe. On the way back to the trailer, he swung into a building supply store that was just about to close, and stocked up on nails and wood and even a fucking hammer. God knows if that broad owns a hammer.

"You were gone a long time. I was about to piss myself." Emma was reading a magazine on the deck among her plants potted in all manner of containers and she looked rather peaceful. Aloe grew from an old tire she'd filled with soil and flowering orchids sprouted from dilapidated crab pots. Bart had to admit the plants were already looking better than when they'd pulled in yesterday afternoon.

"Traffic's a bitch. Good news, though. Got your dinner, and a special treat too!"

Emma's face lit up. "What kind of treat?"

Bart put down paper bags of food in the kitchen but left the hardware in the car. He wasn't sure yet exactly what he wanted to do. He came back outside to lean over Emma. He hefted her right breast and she instinctively reached for his bulge. "You've never had anything like this shit, but you gotta be patient."

Bart pinched her nipple through her shirt and headed inside. Emma wheeled in behind him, nearly clipping his heels. "Don't forget about me, Einstein. And you'd better put on some music or the news of something. All this fucking silence is gonna make me flip my shit."

"Oh yeah?" Bart turned around to pick Emma

up from her wheelchair, but she moved in closer and yanked down his shorts. She worked him expertly and then pulled one of his hands between her legs.

"You're the horniest split-tail I ever seen."

Bart lifted her from the chair and carried her to the bed where they rutted like barnyard animals.

"I thought you had to pee."

"I do. Especially now. Don't want a UTI."

Bart dutifully picked her up and helped her do her business. A few minutes later, they were back in bed, still sweating. Emma reached over to her other bedside nightstand, not the one opposite where she kept her grocery money, and pulled out a stash of green bud.

"I'd almost forgotten I had this," she said. "It's gonna be stale, but at least it's weed." Emma sat up and rolled a joint on her lap.

Bart's eyebrows went up. "Wooeee." This was a nice turn of events.

Emma lit the joint and passed it to Bart after taking a long hit. "I'm starving," she said after they'd finished it off and she'd already begun rolling a second.

"At your service, Boss Lady. You gonna hang here 'til the chow's ready?"

Emma shook her head. "I wanna be in the kitchen with you."

Bart, giddy like a kid, gave her a high five. "You can be my assistant, but you gotta do whatever I say or you're fired."

Emma giggled. "Let's not forget who works for who!"

Bart eased her naked body into the wheelchair. "Don't get uppity or I'll quit."

They both knew he was lying.

"Alright," she said, smoothing her tangled hair with

both hands. "Let's see what's going on with this storm."

Emma wheeled over to the small TV balanced on top of a stained plastic milk crate. The unit was old enough that it came equipped with VHS. She pressed the power button and waited as a local channel came partly into focus, offering fuzzy reruns of "The Golden Girls."

Bart already knew she only got three channels, but they were local and bound to start giving weather reports soon, if they hadn't already begun. He couldn't risk that shit.

"Hey," he said, sidling between her and the screen and flicking off the power with an aggravated poke. "No worries. I got the weather report while I was out. Just a little storm, it'll pass soon. Let's put on some music and enjoy our night."

Classic rock blared from the radio speakers while Bart and Emma passed a joint between them. Bart marinated the meat and Emma dumped the pretzels and bugles into bowls. She admired the whiskey Bart had picked up and didn't seem phased at all by its price. Maybe that was the weed talking.

A nice quiet passed over them and they realized the rain had nearly stopped. Bart poked his head outside. "All right. Mostly clear. That means we can do the steaks on the grill, not in the pan."

"Sounds good," said Emma. "It's propane. You know how to use it, Einstein?"

"Do I know how to use propane? Have you already forgotten what they call me?"

"Thrill Meets Grill, right, stud?" Emma laughed.

After a quick trip to the john, where he pocketed a fifty he found in a band-aid tin in the medicine cabinet, Bart shuffled barefoot to the deck to grill the Flintstonesized T-bones. He hollered over his shoulder. "How you want it cooked?"

"Shhh!" Emma held her index finger against her lips and turned up the radio with her other hand. Joey Naples, a popular regional broadcaster, was running down the latest information released by the National Hurricane Center and then urged his listeners to be prepared.

"Evacuation orders are being given in the Florida Keys as Monroe County emergency managers prepare for Hurricane Patty. Key West International Airport will close Tuesday night, canceling all commercial flights until further notice. A State of Local Emergency was declared for Monroe County on Tuesday afternoon. Traffic is building on the overseas highway as locals and tourists get out of the Keys ahead of an evacuation order. Monroe County Emergency Operations Center Director Martin Booth says, "We're emphatically telling people you must evacuate, you cannot afford to stay on an island with a Category 5 hurricane coming at you. Most of this island chain is only three to five feet above sea level. With the surges we're expecting, this is not the place to be," said Booth. "A visitor evacuation is expected to begin at sunrise on Wednesday. An evacuation for residents also will be issued. The time has yet to be determined. There will be no shelters open in Monroe County."

"Holy fuck," Emma said slowly, as if she were waking up from a dream. "We gotta get out of here."

Bart shrugged. "Okay, but we got plenty of time. We'll leave tomorrow. Storm is still a day out."

Emma shook her head. "Did you know about this?"

"Of course not. That's the weed talking. You're

paranoid. I didn't know nothing 'til now."

"But didn't you see people at the store, on the road, evacuating, getting supplies?"

"Yeah, yeah, of course, but I thought it was just normal storm stuff. You know, the kind where people hunker down and drink for a couple days."

"And you assumed you'd be staying here for that?"

"No, I mean, I don't got to. You can get somebody else to put you on the shitter."

The nonchalant comment had done its work. Emma got quiet and for once didn't seem to have a comeback.

"Look, it's barely even raining now. Let's eat, get some sleep, then we'll bust outta here first thing tomorrow." Bart went back out to the grill. "How you want your steak, Crip?"

Emma followed to the open trailer door.

"Fuck, I can't even think straight. Make it rare. We've gotta hurry and get shit packed. You'll need to go back to the store and get me some stuff to board up with."

"Chill. No worries," he said. "You want this here cow rare, you say? Great. Walk mine past the grill and it's done. The bloodier, the better!"

They dined in front of the old TV, watching Bruce Willis kick ass on Christmas Eve in the Nakatomi Tower. "This is my favorite movie," Emma said more than once. By the time they finished eating, they were too stuffed to clean up. Bart popped a cold one and handed it to Emma, along with a refill on her whiskey.

She was obviously trying to relax, but she kept checking the clock on the kitchen microwave. It was nearing midnight.

"If we're going to get packed and on the road in the morning, we'd better get to bed."

"Sure thing."

"Bart, if we don't board up in the morning, my trailer will be destroyed."

"It's all good. I remember seeing some boards behind a trailer down the street. I'll snag 'em in the morning. Probably take less than fifteen minutes to board up this Taj Mahal. You ready for your pill?"

Emma nodded, softening. "Sorry I freaked out. I'm actually really glad you're here to help me. Plus, I'd just run out of my pills. I'd be in so much pain if you hadn't gotten them, you have no idea. You're so good to me, Bart."

He smiled and handed her a Percocet, which she swallowed without further discussion.

"You want one?" she offered. "Will help you sleep."

"Negatory, they're yours. You'll need em. Besides, I wanna keep an eye on you. Make sure you get to sleep okay."

Bart got up, opened the old freezer door and pulled out a can of orange juice concentrate. He mixed it with some tap water in an empty Tupperware pitcher and poured some in a cup.

While Emma was watching the last minutes of Bruce slobber all over his estranged wife, Bart ground up two more Percosets and added them to the juice.

"Here," he said, handing her the cup, "My gramps always said an OJ a day keeps the hangover away."

Emma looked up with real gratitude in her eyes. She took the cup and drank it all down.

Twenty minutes later, her head hung to the right while she drooled down her shoulder. Bart lit another joint and went over his plan.

PATTYCAKES

Pattycakes Farley spotted her hunky cop within seconds. He sat at a corner of the bar that afforded him a view of the street, the parking lot, and the band. Patty wound her way through the crowd gathered on the covered wooden deck. Their eyes met before she reached him.

Hammond took his time scanning her from top to bottom. It'd been drizzling all day, much to Patty's chagrin, and her walk from the Snatch Patch hadn't been fun.

"You're soaked." He stood and gestured to his bar stool. "Have a seat. What can I get you to drink, Darlin'? Miller Lite, right?" As he waited for her to answer, he pulled napkins from a nearby dispenser and handed them to her.

The polite gesture wasn't lost on Patty. "Thanks, a Lite would be great." She wiped her face with the napkins.

Hammond leaned against the bar until the bartender handed him the beer.

"Wanna head out back? It's closer to the water."

Patty laughed and gestured to her wet clothes.

"The tables have umbrellas," he said. "And there might be more room."

That sounded more intimate, and intimate sounded good to Patty.

Hammond lead the way to a large uncovered deck littered with umbrella tables and plastic chairs. Patty kept her eyes firmly planted on his backside. She liked what she saw and was tempted to grab a handful, but decided to be patient. Her aggressive moves tended to scare away members of the opposite sex.

A band played on a raised stage covered with a palm-frond roof. Their upbeat rhythms kept a pretty big crowd on the dance floor, despite the heavy drizzle.

Hammond put his beer on a wooden railing framing the deck and stood with his arms crossed in front of him. A bright blue awning kept him mostly out of the rain.

"How's this?" he asked.

"Perfect."

Patty thought he looked nervous about where to put his hands. She knew exactly where she wanted those tanned, thick fingers, but Hammond obviously needed some clues.

Patty stood very close and waited. Then she leaned into his side. He was warm and solid. He took a step to put space between them, which Patty quickly filled. He wasn't getting away that easily.

"So, where do you live?" Hammond asked.

Patty wasn't interested in conversation. "Actually, I just moved in at work. The boss keeps these nice rooms for his staff, if they want them." She shifted her stance and leaned against the left side of his chest.

"Oh yeah? Where's that?"

"The Snatch Patch."

She felt him stiffen.

"Easy there, Hoss. I don't bite. Not initially, anyway."

"It's not that. It's just. I didn't know you were a dancer."

"I'm not. I'm a bartender."

Hammond still looked uncomfortable, but Patty pulled his arm around her waist and held it in place.

"You know I can't do this, Darlin'. I'm married." But he didn't pull away and Patty thought she felt him press slightly closer.

She took a big gulp of beer without letting go of his arm. "I don't see your wife here, and besides, we're just friends. Enjoy yourself." Patty swayed her hips to the beat of the music, intentionally grinding her backside against Hammond.

He lowered his head and spoke, his mouth almost against Patty's ear. "Hang on. I'll get us another round."

The closeness of his lips to her skin made her knees weak. She nodded but hated to let him walk away. The beach musicians stopped playing and the members headed to the bar for a few drinks. Patty watched the way they moved through the crowd, confident but aloof. Unwanted memories of a scruffy guitar player she had once known flooded her mind.

Hammond returned with two fresh beers, forcing Patty's mind back to the present. He handed one to her and then offered his elbow. As she took hooked her arm through his, Hammond leaned down and whispered.

"Wanna tell me about it?"

Patty didn't like being caught looking sad. She took a long sip of her beer. "Nope, I'm fine."

She gently laid her head against his arm and felt a strange sensation well up inside that was unfamiliar, long-forgotten. Something like tenderness. She looked up into Hammond's eyes and something unspoken passed between them.

After the band knocked out another reggae dance tune, the rain let up. The dark sky lightened up enough to make visible the bright stars that had been previously hidden by clouds.

Hammond led Patty wordlessly down the dimly lit path, away from the crowd and the noise. The water lapped at the land and painted pictures in Patty's mind of Hammond doing the same to her. He dropped to the small spit of sand and, without waiting for an invitation, she sat sideways with her head cradled against his chest.

"I'm really flattered, Darlin'," he said, "and I won't lie. I'm attracted to you, but nothing can come of it."

She nodded. She felt a bit dizzy. Hammond smelled delectable. It wasn't the scent of cologne, but of man. Just good, solid man.

"So why did you agree to come then, Hoss? Was it really to be my guide to Islamorada?"

"Because I like you. I think you're interesting. And I wanted to make sure you'll be safe during the storm. Also, you're new to the Keys and, if you haven't already figured it out, things work differently here than on the mainland."

Patty laughed. "You're a lousy liar. You came 'cuz you wanna get laid. Admit it, Hoss."

He gently pushed Patty off his lap. "That's not true. I don't mess around."

"You know what I hear?" Patty put her hands on both sides of Hammond's face and made him look at her. "I hear you say that you're married. I hear you say that you aren't a cheater. But you know what I've not heard?" Patty paused. "You've never said that you're happy."

Hammond sighed. "It's complicated."

Patty nestled herself into his lap. They were silent for several minutes, Patty enjoying the feeling of their closeness under the starry sky. She'd moved heaven and earth, not to mention slung bar with her titties hanging out for hours last night, just to be here with him, this guy she barely knew, and she didn't regret a thing.

She felt the regular beat of his heart through his shirt.

"So, how do you like working at The Snatch Patch?" Hammond's lips brushed against Patty's ear as he spoke and she tipped her head closer, savoring the sensation.

"Not sure. Just started."

He leaned back, planting his hands in the sand behind him. "I hear the bartenders are, um, naked up top. Sort of surprised you work there."

She pulled away again. "Why are you surprised?" She covered her breasts protectively with her free hand. "You don't think people want to see my tits?"

"Easy there, Darlin'. Your Irish is showing." Hammond smiled, in spite of her reaction. "The Snatch Patch can be, well, I just took you for someone with a little more of those East Coast street smarts. Just be careful there. Especially since I'm sure any man would love to see your breasts."

"Or woman."

"Or woman."

Patty softened. "Why didn't you say so, Hoss?" She positioned herself in front of him, on her knees in the wet sand. She tried to move slow and sexy like the dancers at work, but the beer wasn't working in her favor. She felt like more of a hockey player than an exotic dancer, but she could tell the effort wasn't lost on

Hammond. Something told her it had been years since a woman had tried to impress him.

Crawling closer, she took his face in her hands and kissed him hard. His grip grew tighter.

"Patty, I've already fucked up enough for one week. This can't happen."

"Shhh," Patty whispered. "No one cares. You're gonna fuck me right here."

Hammond moaned, and closed his eyes, and then painstakingly, regretfully, positioned Patty back into the sand beside him.

"Why don't you tell me what was bothering you back at the tent?"

Patty sighed. This wasn't going the way she wanted at all. "It's not a big deal."

Hammond studied the water. "I guess I can't very well ask you to open up if I don't. All right. Here it is. Yesterday morning I was about to leave for my shift when I realized my gun, radio, and cell phone were all missing. I drove to the station to report it to my captain, and he suspended me."

"He suspended you for that?"

"Yeah well . . ." Hammond rubbed the back of his neck sheepishly. "It's a big deal really. And all my fault because I tend to leave them in my trunk.

"Anyway, we tried my phone first, but it's like it's disappeared from the earth. Whoever took it knows how to disable tracking devices."

"Not to make you feel bad, but who keeps their cell phone in their trunk?"

"You sound like my captain now," Hammond chuckled, still rubbing the back of his neck. "It's a stupid habit, I know. Maybe it's growing up on the island and feeling like I'm safe here, like I don't need to worry. Pretty dumb for someone in my line of work. Anyway, the thing is that whoever broke into my trunk knew that's where I kept all that stuff."

"What did your wife say about all this?" Patty was trying to match the gravity of Hammond's tone, and sound serious, but the beer was getting to her head and she slurred the word "wife."

"Oh," Hammond looked down. "Carrie wanted to avoid the hurricane so she packed up and left today."

"Why didn't you go with her?"

"You know, the house. Someone had to board up windows, trim the palms, stock up on water. Stock up on beer. Meet a pretty young thing."

Patty liked that last part. The conversation was starting to come back around to where she wanted it.

"Your turn, Darlin'" said Hammond. "Tell me what was getting you down back there."

This wasn't the version of "I'll Show Your Mine If You Show Me Yours" that Patty wanted to play, but it felt good to talk to someone. It'd been months, maybe years, since she'd had this kind of intimacy with anyone.

"All right, but we're keeping it short. And then we're getting more drinks and changing the topic completely. It was those dumb musicians back there. The summer I graduated high school, I fell in love at a beach concert on the Cape. The lead singer. The following three months were a blur. Lots of sex, loud concerts. He was a dick sometimes, but I was happy, Hoss, really happy. Blissful. I was young, dumb, and full of cum, as they say, and I had no doubt that Danny—that was his name—was the one. I thought he felt the same way. But when I finally got up the nerve to tell him, at the end of the summer, he told me he had a fiancée. This chick had flown home to Sacramento back in May to take care of her mother who'd had back surgery or some shit. He said he was sorry that he'd gotten carried away. Carried away. Can you fucking believe it? Three months of being together all the time, no mention of a girlfriend, much less a fiancé, and he calls it getting carried away."

Hammond was quiet a moment, obviously giving her his full attention.

"Did you ever tell her?"

"Tell who?"

"The fiancé? Seems like she ought to know what a scum he was."

"Naw, fuck her. She can have him."

It had been nearly twelve years since that stupid, wonderful, terrible summer, and Patty had never told anyone the story. Here she was, with a married man she'd known a day, spilling her guts. And then she realized it wasn't the musicians that reminded her of that summer, it was being here with a married guy. Once again wanting what she couldn't have.

Better to not care.

The sky suddenly darkened again, shrouding the stars behind heavy clouds. They both knew what was coming, so Hammond helped Patty up, going so far as to playfully brush some sand off her butt. She didn't mind. On the way back, the rain resumed its steady beat as they both ran back to the covered deck of the Lorelei.

"How 'about another Lite?" Hammond asked.

"I can't believe I'm saying this, but no. I've got a special event tonight at the Snatch Patch, and I gotta go get ready."

"Darlin', about that musician. I'm sorry that

happened to you."

Patty shrugged. "It was a long time ago."

"Your boss is taking care of you, right? I know the building connected to The Snatch Patch is pretty fortified, but you gotta make sure you have lots of clean drinking water."

"Hoss, it's a bar."

"Fair enough." Hammond laughed.

They made their way through the crowded bar, now packed with rowdy locals who decided to stay and party through the storm. Standing at the far end of the bar, Patty recognized the bouncer from The Snatch Patch. He was laughing loudly as he handed some cash to the bartender. Their eyes met only briefly before Hammond took her hand in his.

"Let's make a run for it. I'll give you a ride."

They hurried across the parking lot. Hammond opened the passenger side door and Patty slid inside. She immediately liked the way it smelled and felt. Empty Dairy Queen blizzard cups littered the front seat and he mumbled his apologies as he tossed them in the back.

"You should see Lucille. This is nothing compared to her."

"She your car?"

Patty grinned. "Yeah. My VW. My baby."

"Where is she now?"

"Getting fixed up, right around the corner. They should have her ready tomorrow."

"Good deal. I hope she survives the storm."

"What about you, Hoss? Are you going to be okay?"

"Yeah, my house is pretty used to being beaten up. It was built to outlast hurricanes."

"But you don't have a cell phone."

"Got a land line."

"God, you ARE old."

Hammond laughed. "I can give you the number if you want it."

"You sure you want me calling your land line?"

"Look, if you want me to tell you that I am willing to cheat on my wife, no, I won't say that. But if you want me to tell you we're happy, that the marriage is strong, well, that's not true either."

"So where does that leave me?"

Hammond pulled into the small front parking lot of The Snatch Patch. "Just give me time, Darlin'. We have some time, right? You'll be in town for a while?"

The plan had been to rescue Lucille and get the hell out of Dodge before the storm. Patty could always come back in a couple weeks. But then she'd have to cut ties with The Snatch Patch, and she didn't really know where else to get a job if she came back. And what if she came back and this cop was still not going to fuck her? Patty sensed the early stirring of an old familiar feeling that she didn't want to deal with. She actually liked this guy. And that was a bad idea.

No, she'd better get Lucille ASAP and get out of the Keys, find her spot in the sun somewhere else. She could stay and ride out the storm at The Patch, but the truth was Patty didn't much like the idea of working there for very long. She could already feel beneath the leering men and rude boss—which she didn't particularly mind—something darker that she couldn't quite put her finger on.

"Listen," Hammond said, leaning in, face-to-face with Patty as if reading her mind. "I can't tell you any more than this, but you gotta keep your wits about you at that place. It's been under investigation a number of times for some bad stuff. I mean BAD stuff. We've never been able to prove it. But I don't like you going there. So, could you do me a favor and check in with me after your shift? Or maybe tomorrow?"

"Okay, Dad," Patty laughed.

"I'm serious." And he was. Hammond's brows were furrowed and his mouth was set in a thin line.

"All right," said Patty, surprising herself. She couldn't believe all the things she was doing that weren't at all like her. "I'm a big girl though. I can handle myself. But I'll call you because you know I want a piece of this ass."

Hammond leaned back, laughing and blushing at the same time. Patty got out of the car, pleased with herself. Pleased that she could make this older, handsome cop feel good.

The rain was coming in sheets when Patty got to her room. The hurricane party started in about an hour and she still had a lot to do. After a hot a shower in the communal hall bathroom, she managed to put on some mascara, eyeliner, and lipstick in the foggy mirror. Then she put on a cute pair of skin-tight leggings she'd been saving for a special occasion. They were embedded with silver sparkles that glittered softly in the mirror.

Downstairs, men had been arriving over the course of the past hour, some with bags or small suitcases, hurled in from the bad storm raging outside. Patty's stomach climbed into her throat and refused to leave. There was something different about this party, she could feel it. The whole thing about a hurricane party was that no one left until the storm was over, and suddenly that didn't seem like such a great idea.

Carla was topless behind the bar, and two girls wearing thongs and six-inch heels spoke with Sam near the stage.

"What the hell's wrong?" Carla asked. "You look like death."

Patty plopped onto a stool and covered her face with both hands. "I don't feel good."

Carla rested her elbows on the bar. "Sam told me you're working the floor tonight. You nervous?"

"I think I'm gonna puke." Patty wiped her forehead with a bar napkin. "Is it hot in here?"

Carla poured a shot and nudged Patty's arm. "Stop worrying. It's not as bad as you think." Patty tossed back a Fireball. "It's really no big deal unless you make it one." Patty thought that made good sense. She didn't mind delivering drinks, it was the idea of being stuck inside for days with a lot of strange men that was giving her a weird feeling. Or maybe it was something else.

"Take one of these." Carla slid a small pill across the bar that sailed like a hockey puck until it stopped in front of Patty. "It'll calm your nerves."

Patty watched Carla swallow one and then followed suit.

"What is this?"

"It's a little miracle that keeps you sane." Carla tipped her head in the direction of the stage. "Looks like the boss wants you."

Sam waved Patty over and then checked his watch. He wiped his nose with the heel of a hand while she crossed the dimly lit room.

"Here's the deal, anything goes tonight. My clients wanna sample the goods, you let 'em."

Patty took a step back and shook her head, but Sam reached out and put his arm protectively around her shoulder.

"It couldn't be easier. They ask for a little of this, a little of that, and you get rich." Sam put his index finger under her chin and tipped her head upwards. "Listen, you're free to leave any time. But if you leave, you leave. You pack your things and go."

Patty heard the wind roar outside as if in answer.

Sam leaned in. "Look, I'm gonna pay you five Ben Franklins just to be here." He smiled and pulled her closer. "The men, they'll pay you even more. Some girls leave my special events with thousands of dollars just falling out of their panties."

Patty cleared her throat and tried to smile.

"Speaking of, take off those goddamn leggings. Tonight you're wearing a thong."

"A thong?"

"Carla will set you up."

Patty was speechless. All of her Irish fire flew out of her. Sample the goods? Was she going to be grabbed a lot? Or was she expected to actually . . . participate? She was getting a sinking feeling this was going to be more than a couple handfuls of ass being squeezed.

Patty only nodded. She was afraid if she spoke she'd throw up on her boss's off-white gabardine slacks. Sam patted her backside and nudged her toward the ladies' room. "Now don't just stand there like a bobble head. Make my guests happy."

Patty walked back to the bar shaking her head. "I don't think I can do this, Carla. I'm gonna puke."

"Nobody's gonna make you, sweetheart. If you don't feel good, just tell Sam you're leaving."

It was a dirty trick, but it worked.

"Good," said Carla. "Here you go." She handed Patty a black thong from the depths of her big, black bag.

"Goddammit!" Patty slapped the back of a bar stool, sending it spinning. "I'll be right back." She grabbed the underwear and stomped to the restroom, slamming the door behind her.

Ten minutes later, Patty teetered out of the ladies' room in just the thong and her heels, feeling very much like she'd left a Walmart changing room too early.

Sam came over to inspect. "You look like a goddamn Kindergarten teacher in those things!" Sam smacked his forehead with an open palm. "Somebody get Pippy Longstocking here some real shoes!"

Carla bent behind the bar and dug out a pair of hot pink, five-inch heels from a black leather bag and slammed them onto the bar. "At least try to make it look like you want the job," she hissed to Patty. "He's doin' you a huge favor."

Patty yanked off the shoes she had been wearing and tossed them behind the bar, not caring where they landed. It required Herculean effort to cram her wide feet and extra-long talons into the impossibly narrow heels. When both feet had been successfully wedged in, Patty took a tentative step and winced. "Ouch! These are way too small, Carla."

"Tough shit," Sam spoke over his shoulder as he walked toward the office.

Patty leaned against the bar, holding onto a stool for balance. Her toes were already numb as she teetered from stool to stool. Twice she rolled her left ankle. "I can't walk in these fucking things."

Carla shrugged. "Just hold on to a table and you'll be fine." Patty lurched forward and then flailed her arms behind her in what would have been an impressive backstroke had she been in a pool.

"Better yet," yelled Carla from across the bar, "Grab hold of a big ole dick."

A group of twenty-five or thirty men had gathered. The music was loud and the lighting was low. Patty did her best to look sexy. She tried to mimic the moves of Sam's other girls, but her confidence was nowhere to be found. None of the men had given her a second glance. "What the hell am I doing here?" she thought. "I'm not cut out for this shit."

Her thoughts were suddenly interrupted by a slimy voice behind her.

"How 'bout a lap dance?"

Patty's reaction time was slowed—must be the pill Carla had given her. She turned around the best she could. "Who, me?"

The man laughed. "Yeah, you. Pop a squat and show me whatcha got." He was seated in an overstuffed chair, patting his ample-sized lap with a chubby, hairy hand.

"Aw, Jeez."

His backside barely squeezed onto the wide, upholstered cushion. He patted his lap a second time, as if calling the family dog. Definitely not fuckable. But Patty smiled and wobbled over. At least she could get off her feet.

No sooner had Patty straddled his thick thighs when the man's clammy hands went to her breasts. He helped himself to all of the flesh he could get as she ground her crotch against his in rhythm to the music.

To avoid looking at his pocked, saggy face and the sweat stains spreading from his pits, Patty threw back her head and pretended to enjoy his touch. The man's rough hands slid down her bare back. He snapped her thong before smacking her left butt cheek. It was impossible not to notice that he'd popped a boner, and his reaction stirred a perverse sense of pride in Patty. She'd managed to make him rock hard with little more than a few hip grinds. She felt powerful.

The Sweat Monster cupped one of her breasts and slipped it into his mouth. Patty closed her eyes and continued to grind. She tried to imagine it was Hammond but failed. "How about a drink?" she said. "I'll be right back. Don't you even think about moving." Patty gave her best fake smile.

He winked and tucked a twenty into her G-string. She cringed from the numbing pain in her feet as she staggered to the bar, frustrated for not learning how to walk in heels like a normal woman. Patty's nipple protested the goings-on and she absent-mindedly wiped it with the back of her hand. "Carla, I need something strong!"

But Carla wasn't behind the bar. In fact, no one was. On the other side of the room, Carla had been called to the corner to discuss something with Boss and another dude, a sort of silver fox who looked a bit more put together than some of the other guys here. Patty needed something to get through this, another pill.

Carla's big black bag was stuffed under the counter as usual, full of all sorts of party tricks, no doubt. Never one to split hairs about other people's property, Patty ducked down and rummaged through the bag. She found yet another pair of back-up heels, two more G-strings in hot pink and bright yellow, and a little orange bottle that said Ibuprofen, but which she was sure was full of something else. She picked it up and was about to open the tab when she saw a flip phone beneath it. Who the hell has a flip phone anymore? Laughing, she picked it up, opened it , marveling, and quickly shut it again. She had thrown it back into the bottom of the bag when she saw the little window screen light up. 1 TEXT: HAMMOND.

Hammond.

Breathlessly, Patty opened the phone again. A string of texts between Carla and Hammond. Was there another Hammond in town? Could be? But as she was reading them, she started to realize that Carla and Hammond were talking about police stuff, about new updates in a human trafficking investigation, and even some photo evidence.

Patty clicked on the photo. It brought up a picture of a dark-haired girl she'd never seen before, no more than twenty, with a black eye, lying unconscious in a hospital bed, haggard and dirty-faced. The text said: POSSIBLE HUMAN TRAFFICKING VICTIM. IN COMA. KEY WEST. LAST SEEN WORKING LORELEI. She clicked back but that only brought her to the full photo gallery. The camera held about a dozen pictures, most of a middle-aged woman and what looked like a teenage kid. Patty gasped as she recognized Hammond. It looked like a recent photo of him sitting in a diner, eating pancakes, and giving a straight smile to the camera.

She went back to the texts. In one of them Hammond wrote: LOUIS, BREAKFAST AT OUR USUAL?

It was then Patty realized it wasn't Carla's phone at all. It belonged to someone named Louis. And Louis was friends with Hammond. HER Hammond. Hammond, whose phone had also been stolen.

Patty was shaking. The drugs and alcohol were making her tired and dizzy, and all she could think was she had to get out of there and call Hammond. But of course she couldn't, he didn't have a cell. And there was a wicked storm outside, she could hear it. She would need to just get through tonight, keep her wits about her, and then get the hell out as soon as she could. But what if that wasn't for a couple days? Well, she would have to figure it out.

Patty did the one thing that she knew she could do. She forwarded the whole conversation to her cell, which was locked away back in her room.

"Hey there, Red, stop fiddling in your purse, get me a drink, and come back and sit on my face."

Patty jerked up.

Of course. It was the man who had slobbered all over her. He had pried his fat ass from the chair and followed her to the bar. He was waving two twenties in the air. Patty poured him a tumbler of whiskey and said she'd be right over. A quick lap dance had been bad enough. Patty didn't want to have to do more than that, but feared she would probably have to.

Carla was nowhere to be seen. Probably in the back room doing coke or whatever it was that Carla did to keep going. Patty thought she had the right idea. There was no way she was going to get through this as she was. She reached into Carla's bag and pulled out the bottle and popped one.

"Just what the fuck do you think you're doing?"

Carla reared up next to Patty, her cat eyes blazing.

Patty put the pills on the counter as if giving up stolen goods.

"I can't fucking do this. I need at least one more."

"All right, but don't ever go through my shit again." Carla snatched the bottle of pills and dumped two out onto Patty's hand. Take em both, you stupid wench."

"Jeez, testy much?"

But Patty knew enough to know she'd struck a nerve, and something really shady was going on with Carla. Maybe she ought to say something to the boss, but then again, she just wanted to stop thinking. She wanted to stop feeling scared. She took both pills and made her way back to the Sweat Hog. He'd managed to squeeze his massive bulk back into the same chair as before. He was waiting for her like they were on a date.

She cringed as his sticky wet hand caressed her ass but she stuck out her backside as if to welcome the touch. Another hand came from behind and found its way to her right breast. Patty leaned against the large body behind her and closed her eyes. She dropped her arms to her sides while the stranger's hands continued their aggressive inventory of her body.

And then something happened. All the magic kicked in. Wave after wave of bliss, of pleasure, of relaxation. Never before had she felt so peaceful and happy. It was the best she'd felt in a very long time and she didn't want it to end. It didn't matter who was groping her, so long as she could keep feeling like that.

"How much did you see, little girl?" he asked gruffly in her ear.

"A lot," said Patty distantly. And it was mostly true. The room was full of noise, a loud bass pumped up to an almost painful level. What she had heard was, "How much do you like me, little girl?" and she had answered with that distant part of her brain that still knew what she was supposed to say to make everyone happy.

DAY THREE

HAMMOND

Hammond woke on the sofa to the sound of driving rain and the high whine of storm winds. He could hear it howling outside. He clicked on the news without even getting up. The morning newscaster said the storm had increased in strength and evacuation would be mandatory. With most areas less than seven feet above sea level, the Keys were vulnerable to storm surge flooding.

"Winds can reach 157 miles per hour or higher," the newscaster said. "People and pets can be in danger from flying debris, even indoors."

So, Patty had been upgraded to a cat five. "Probably going to lose power, maybe water," Hammond said to himself.

The storm was growing in feverish size every twelve hours. It'd gone from a Cat 2 to a 3 to a 4, and now they were saying a 5, the biggest hurricane category possible. He recalled how back in 1992, Hurricane Andrew uprooted palms. smashed boats against the sea wall, and tossed dump trucks about like Tonka toys. That had been the worst storm to ravage the Keys in his lifetime and it had taken years for the islands to recover. And now another one was looking them straight in the eye. This was that rare situation when even the police could do nothing but sit and wait it out. Hammond knew that as soon as wind speeds exceeding 40 mph, even emergency responders don't respond. The risks are too great. He also knew that most people just didn't understand that fact and assumed that a call to 911 will always bring help. Hurricanes were the teachers of many truths. Most of them deadly ones.

The weather models predicted that the Keys had less than twelve hours to batten down the hatches before Patty made full landfall. Residents who decided to stay were warned to gather emergency supplies in preparation for the inevitable. Hammond listened as the anchorman ticked off the basics: water, flashlight, batteries, canned goods, medications, first aid kit, and a weather radio. In his experience, people never stored enough water. They overlooked the fact that in addition to drinking it, they'd need water to cook, flush toilets, and perhaps wash cuts and scrapes made by broken glass. One gallon of water per person, per day, for six days, was Hammond's formula and he'd made it through plenty of storms without running out.

Hammond's parents had never believed in evacuating under any circumstances. His dad was a builder, and their home was fortified with every sort of hurricane-resistant building material available. There'd been a few hairy moments during Hurricane Andrew, but Hammond's house always came out the other side unscathed. His mom used to say that their house was like their marriage. It might get tested now and again, but it always held rock solid.

Hammond reflected on the previous night. He'd grown painfully overwhelmed with guilt about nearly giving into Patty's advances. He was sure his father had never cheated on his mom, in spite of the fact that he probably had plenty of opportunities while serving overseas. Hammond berated himself for losing control and promised to redouble his efforts to get his relationship with Carrie back on track—he had made a promise to love and honor his wife and he was going to see it through. That's what marriage was about.

"Stay here with me," Hammond had said as he'd softly come up behind Carrie in their bedroom as she packed to leave. She pulled lacy panties from a top dresser drawer—delicates Hammond had definitely never seen before. "This house is a fortress, it's going to be fine. I've got everything boarded up, we have lots of food and stuff to drink. We can play board games like we used to. You always liked Monopoly."

Carrie stuffed a handful of panties into her bag and sighed.

"Oh, Chris," breathed Carrie. She balled up more panties to stick in her bag. "I need a break anyway. I think WE need a break."

"What does that mean?"

"Don't act surprised."

"What are you saying, Carrie?

She kept shoving clothing into her bag.

"Are you saying you're leaving me? As opposed to just evacuating?"

"I'm just going to my mom's. It's just a break. It'll be good for us. I'm sorry you got suspended, but I've heard that . . . that you aren't doing a very good job of being a cop."

She closed the panty drawer and moved to the second one down where she kept pajamas. They were soft and thin and silky, and they seemed to belong to a foreign princess who would never, in a million years, let someone like Hammond touch her.

"Who told you that?"

"Just . . . I just heard it." Carrie continued to pack, not making eye contact. "I'm almost thirty-five. I have to think about what I want." She paused. "Like, kids. I think I wanna have kids."

Hammond got quiet. This was a sensitive topic. They slept in different rooms, didn't even share goodbye kisses anymore. And she was talking about kids.

"Only, not with you."

It had felt like a dousing with ice water.

Now, lying on the sofa, he wanted to be mad at Carrie, hell, he was mad at Carrie. Who was she talking to on the force that was badmouthing him? He knew what the other guys thought of him, but it pissed him off to imagine one of them talking him down to his wife.

Then there was Patty. Patty, who he'd nearly kissed. Nearly done much more than kiss. Truth was, he couldn't get Patty off his mind.

Maybe he could invite her to stay with him. This was much safer than that sinister back-end of The Snatch Patch.

But that was way beyond the realm of appropriate. He was still married, goddammit.

Hammond stood and stretched, noticing that his belly stuck out further than he remembered. The lack of sexual activity and female attention over the past few years had provided little incentive to worry about his physique. He considered his reflection in the full-length mirror on the back of the bathroom door and was more than a little disappointed in the view. After a quick rummage through the laundry room, which doubled as his closet, he was suited up for a run. He ate an over-ripe banana in three bites and tossed the brown-spotted peel into his wife's compost bin then hit the dusty treadmill in the corner of the living room, watching through the window as the storm took over his backyard.

By the time Hammond finished a fifteen-minute run, he had decided to call Patty. He looked around for his cell before remembering it had gone the way of the Dodo Bird. "Fuck!" He banged his fist on the counter. He should have given Patty his land line. At least he'd written down her number before they'd parted last night.

As he picked up the phone from the cradle, he noticed the message alert was blinking. Weird. He hadn't heard any calls come in last night. He checked the volume. Sure enough the ringer had been muted. "Why the hell do you do this shit, Carrie?" he said out loud.

He clicked the button to hear the messages.

Hammond had sunk down into a chair by the time they'd both played.

His dear friend was dead. There was a police investigation, Matt had gone missing then returned home, and Stella was frightened. Jesus Christ.

He cried briefly and hated the sound of it. Then he called Stella back.

An hour later, Hammond pulled into the Callahan's. The seven-mile drive had taken so long because of high winds and flying debris. Trees, trash cans, and coconuts were being tossed around. He made his way carefully up the outdoor stairs, holding tight to the railing, up to the front door.

"Over here!" yelled Stella.

Louis' wife was seated on the enclosed porch adjacent to the living room, smoking a cigarette solemnly. She looked a bit worse for wear.

Hammond still couldn't get his mind around it. Louis was one of those guys who seemed like he would live forever.

He sat down. "What happened?"

"Didn't they tell you down at the precinct? Like I said on the phone, Louis died, just down there." She pointed with her cigarette to the rocking dock below.

"He was sitting downstairs in his chair by the dock," Stella explained. "No witnesses. Neighbors heard nothing. I was out there," she flicked her wrist to the side of the canal that opened to the ocean. "Fishing all morning. He was asleep when I left. He was dead when I got back."

"Mother of God," whispered Hammond. His cop senses kicked into gear. Something very old, over a decade old, was stirring in him. The reason he got into this field of thankless work in the first place.

"Yeah." She looked up at him with big, gray, dead eyes. She'd been through hell and back and he hadn't been here.

"First, I'm so sorry. If I had known, I'd have been here in a heartbeat. Second, you gotta tell me who's working the case."

"Well, I wanted it to be you, but I suppose you don't do murder investigations, that's a special squad or something, right?"

"Right. And even if I was Homicide, I'd be removed. Conflict of interest."

"Well, it's a nice guy named Lopez, got me out of

a tight spot so I'm trying to be patient with him. Other guy is Tom Williams or Williamson. Something like that. He's more of your typical prick. They came over yesterday. He says it's an open and shut case."

Hammond put his hand out on Stella's and she shivered a little bit but let him keep it there. He was thinking.

"I managed to get the house boarded up," she said. "Matt helped me. But I didn't have the money or time or materials to get this porch ready. So, I'm just gonna to sit here and watch the storm until the screening stars to rip apart. Then I'm gonna go in, watch movies with Matt 'til the power goes out, and then maybe sleep for a few days."

"You got enough water?"

Stella shook her head. "It's been slim pickins."

"Well, good thing I brought over a couple tanks for you."

Stella's eyes brightened slightly. "Thanks, Chris. I'm glad you're here."

"I'll bring em up in a little while."

She nodded, thinking. "So, where have you been?"

He signed heavily. "I've been on administrative leave for two days, since Monday morning."

She blinked hard. "Oh shit. What happened?"

"Someone stole my gun. They also took my cell and police radio, but my captain was more pissed off about the gun." Hammond's face was red. "Understandable."

"How'd that happen?"

Hammond told Stella about waking up Monday morning to find everything missing from his trunk.

The wind was blowing hard enough to rattle the porch and the canal waters were rising uncomfortably high. Hammond said, "Look, Stella, I want to bring you and Matt over to my place. It's better fortified, farther from the water."

"All right," Stella sighed. "I'll think about it."

For the rest of the afternoon, Hammond tried his best to get Stella and Matt to make a break for it to his house, but Stella—alternately glassy eyed, angry, then calm and coherent—felt strongly that she didn't want to leave the house.

"We're safer here than out there on the road at this point," she said, putting out her third chain-smoked cigarette. "You're welcome to stay if you want."

Hammond sensed that that was it, the end of the conversation.

Matt was in the kitchen pouring milk over a bowl of sugary-sweet cereal. It wasn't like him. He was usually all about protein smoothies and fresh fruit. Stella was sitting in the living room by a boarded window with an old issue of *People* magazine on her lap, smoking. She had stopped apologizing for filling the boarded-up house with smoke. That wasn't like her either. But Hammond understood. Sometimes you just need something to get you through.

"How's your mom?" Hammond leaned against the fridge, and watched Louis' son dump pink and blue marshmallow cereal into a plastic bowl.

"She's got a funeral to pay for."

Matt chucked the empty box on the kitchen counter, rattling a stack of dirty dishes. He yanked open a drawer, rifled through, and produced a gravy ladle, which he dropped into his cereal bowl. Milk splashed over the sides and onto the counter.

"I guess it's good you're here. It's going to be tough on her without Louis."

"Oh, so my dad treated us like royalty?" Matt suddenly pushed the cereal bowl away, sending another cascade of milk onto the counter. "I can't wait to get the hell off this stupid island."

Hammond was quiet. He wanted Matt to keep talking.

"He made her miserable when he was alive and now that he's dead, people expect us to act like we're so sad and we miss him and blah, blah, blah! It's a bunch of crap!" Matt kicked the baseboard and slammed his clenched fist on the counter. "I'm glad he's dead!"

It hurt Hammond to hear that kind of thing about Louis, but he knew his friend hadn't been a stellar father since retiring. Maybe even before that. The gin had taken over and transformed Louis into a different man. Unfortunately, anger has a way of clouding the good memories and magnifying the bad.

"I don't blame you, Matt. Your dad could have done better." Hammond began cleaning up the counter.

"What? You're not going to tell me that I need to be more respectful?"

Hammond continued to wipe the counter and then attacked the pile of dirty dishes. "Nope."

"How come?"

"Cuz you're right. Your dad didn't pay enough attention to you. You have every right to be angry." The sink filled with hot, soapy water. Hammond scrubbed off old, dried scrambled eggs and macaroni and cheese, placing the clean dishes in the drying rack on the counter.

Matt grabbed a dishtowel and began to help. "I

can't believe you're not yelling at me."

Hammond shrugged. "Not my job."

"You don't have to wash those, you know. I was supposed to do it yesterday."

"No biggie. When these are done, I want to show you some stuff your dad was working on. Might help you understand him a bit more."

Matt tried to sound nonchalant. "Can you show me now?"

"One thing at a time, kid." Hammond flicked soapy dishwater at Matt. "I'll finish these while you take a shower. You smell like a locker room. And I don't know how long we're going to have clean water piping in."

The look on Matt's face brought forth a sharp pang of loneliness for Louis. They looked nothing alike, but something of Louis had definitely shaped the boy. Matt finally nodded and headed off to the shower.

Hammond took a deep breath and sent up a silent prayer for his friend.

When the kitchen was in order, Hammond brought the tanks of water in from the car, nearly knocked over by the wind. Stella was right: they'd all have to ride the storm out here. He then checked each of the boarded windows for weaknesses until Matt got out of the shower.

Within the hour, all three of them were gathered in the living room. "A few months back," Hammond said to Stella, "your husband went to my lieutenant, a guy named Rice, asking for some help on a case involving a runaway who he thought might have been trafficked."

"Wait a minute." Stella put out her cigarette and for the first time in hours, didn't immediately light another one. "Louis was working?"

Hammond chose his words carefully. "Louis was taking on work here and there as a private investigator."

"What?"

"Yeah, he kept it from both of you because it was dangerous. And I think because he was trying to make some money on the side, to make up for . . . you know."

Stella rolled her eyes. "Drinking his damn pension every month?"

"Yeah," Hammond looked down, ashamed for Louis.

Stella shook her head and began to pace the floor.

"I think you should know this. But it's some dark stuff. Is it okay if I continue?"

Stella glanced at Matt, who nodded. "Tell us," she said and sat down.

Chris continued. "Rice agreed to look into the missing girl but then came back right away saying that she'd simply left town. She was eighteen, so legally an adult. She'd been making ends meet at the Lorelei, bussing or bar-backing or something. You know, like a lot of kids do."

"What was her name?" Matt asked.

"Geraldine. The guy who runs the Lorelei, the one your dad talked to, called her Gerry."

"I remember," said Matt. "She hung out once in a while. Then everyone said she'd gone to Jacksonville or something."

"Hung out?" asked Stella.

Matt's face got a little red. "Yeah, just, you know. Around."

"And you didn't hear anything different?" asked Hammond. "Like she'd been taken?"

Matt startled and hugged a couch pillow to his chest. "No, nothing like that."

"Was she hanging out with anyone that could have maybe meant her harm?"

Matt got quiet, thinking. He shook his head. "I don't know."

"Well, your father was never able to get very far with his investigation. Gerry was from the Midwest and her mother was using every resource she had to find her. She'd run away a couple years before and stayed hidden because she wanted to. The mother had gotten word that her daughter was down here but the police were no help at all. That includes me, I guess."

Hammond paused to listen to the storm outside. The hurricane was getting stronger.

"Runaways isn't my beat, but you know, we're all guilty when the department fails those who rely on us. Somehow, the mother ended up contacting Louis." Hammond watched Stella and Matt exchange looks of disbelief. He knew how it sounded.

"Louis went back to my lieutenant for any leads and was shot down hard. But he couldn't let it go. He continued to investigate privately. Did his own digging. Found out a number of young girls from around here had just sort of vanished. Most of them went unnoticed, they were runaways and their parents didn't care. Or didn't know where they'd run to in the first place. But this girl's parent cared, and Louis cared."

"Wait a just one damn second." Stella rolled up the *People* magazine and looked like she might squeeze it back in to pulp. "I lived with Louis. He got up mid-afternoon, drank the day away, then went out to a bar or something, and came back and drank some more. Once in a while he got breakfast with you at the Cholesterol Hut when I was working so he could get a cheap meal. That was his life."

"I know it looked like that. And he really did have a drinking problem." Hammond searched the faces of his captive audience. Stella was red-faced and angry, ready for battle. Matt hugged a tattered throw pillow, looking at the floor, but Hammond saw tears collected in the corners of his downcast eyes. "Louis was an addict. His mind was addled and I think in part that's why he couldn't get farther with this case than he did. Hell, he talked to me about it every single time we'd get together, but I didn't take it all that seriously *because* Louis was such a mess. Thought he was chasing rainbows. But let me ask you this Stella: did you go to bed before him?"

"Every night. Louis was a night owl." She rolled her eyes again. "But what do you expect from someone who doesn't get up until three or four in the afternoon?"

Matt nodded in silent agreement.

"And what about his study? You ever been through his study?"

"I tried to clean it once. Papers everywhere. He didn't like that. Said he wanted things where they were. Even when I begged him to show me our bank account stuff, he kept saying, soon, Stella, soon. Now look what a fucking mess we're in. You know he took most of his pension upfront? I'm going to be living on a widow's pension minus a lot, and I don't know how we're going to send Matt to college. I mean what the fuck!"

Matt's face went pale. "It's okay, Mom. I know you can't afford it. Don't worry about me."

Stella's stone face started to tremble and fall. Her lip quivered and her eyes were lined in angry tears.

"Stella," Hammond said softly. "We'll make sure Matt gets taken care of, one way or another. But what I'm trying to tell you is, I think your husband was on to something. He, I don't know, found something out. And someone got scared."

"But that's the thing, Chris. Louis killed himself. That's what I really think, in my heart of hearts. He got a concussion Sunday night, nearly killed my son by driving them both into the mangroves, was told explicitly that with a concussion, alcohol could kill him, promised me he'd stop, but as soon as he got his hands on some, he drank half a bottle of gin." She lit another cigarette and took a long drag. "So even if some really clever person decided to put that bottle there, it was Louis who picked it up."

"Matt and Louis had a car accident Sunday night?"

"Yep."

Chris turned to Matt.

"You went to the hospital?"

"Yeah. In Tavernier."

Chris was quiet for a moment. "Did you see any officers there?"

Matt shrugged. "No, I don't think so."

Chris leaned in. "Matt, this is very important. Did you tell anyone about your dad's concussion? Especially someone who knew about Louis' drinking problem?"

"Everyone knew about Louis' drinking problem." Stella nearly spat.

Matt ran his hands through his hair and looked away.

"Matt?" Hammond insisted. Did you tell anyone?"

Matt fumbled in his pocket and brought out his phone. "Um," he said, scrolling through his texts awkwardly. "No, I don't think so."

Matt's fumbling gave Hammond an idea. "Hey, where is Louis' phone?"

"He hardly ever used it, but he kept a flip phone for emergencies. It was usually in his office," Stella said. "Why?"

Hammond shook his head. "I don't have any evidence either way, yet. Rice is a nasty son-of-a-bitch and I wouldn't put it past him to have something to do with all of this. But Louis used to text me updates on the investigation. It took him forever with that flip phone, but he liked to use it. So, I'm looking at Sunday night. My phone is stolen. Louis dies the next morning. What if someone got a hold of my phone and found out that Louis knew something they didn't want him to?"

Matt got up and stared across the canal through a slot in the window.

Stella sat up straight. "Are you saying you think someone wanted Louis dead?"

"Matt, can you think of anything else from Sunday night?" Hammond asked. "Anything unusual?"

Matt shook his head, didn't make eye contact, and remained silent.

"Okay, well the good news is we have a good couple of days to scour Louis' study," Hammond continued. "The bad news is that if someone did convince Louis to drink on Monday, it's going to be a couple days before we can do anything about it."

$\mathcal{B}$ART

Bart wadded up the wet diaper and chucked it across the room. It landed on top of an already overflowing trash can.

"Three points!"

He pulled up a clean adult diaper around Emma's waist.

"You fucking stink. Nothing worse than a smelly twat."

He checked the time on his cell and then glanced back at Emma. She was unconscious again. The Percocet was doing its job: giving him the fix he needed—and keeping Emma dead to the world while he figured out what to do. He loved the simplicity of it all. But God, he hated Tiny.

His cousin had called late last night, asking where the fuck he'd got to, and Bart, knowing better than to lie, said he was still with the chick he picked up Monday.

"Oh yeah? She that easy?"

"What can I say, she's good to go."

"Well, look, that's fucking great, but I got an even better deal for you. My guy Sam wants us for this hurricane party."

"Yeah?" Bart decided to play dumb about the whole thing.

"Nothing less than three days of all the pussy and

blow you want, you prick."

"Oh yeah, how much?"

"Two thousand a head."

"You know I don't got that kind of dough."

"That's the thing. Sam will let you in for free. All you have to do is fuck this chick."

"All I gotta do is fuck a chick? That's how I pay Sam?" Bart rolled his eyes.

"Yeah, fuck you, I can hear you rolling your eyes. It's a thing we do." Bart trailed away a little. "I haven't brought you in before because you have to be one of Sam's guys, okay. But he said you could come, lucky bastard. So come."

Bart was afraid to cross his cousin, he'd done it before and it hadn't turned out pretty. But he'd had a plan forming: keep Emma drugged up a couple days, get all her money together, and as soon as the storm passed, take her car, dump it at the state line, and get the fuck out of Dodge. If he didn't show up at the party tonight, Tiny would come looking for him as soon as the storm passed. If he did go tonight, he'd be trapped in The Snatch Patch for days while everything got fucked up with the Emma plan.

It sucked that Tiny was where all the fun was. All the blow, all the girls, all the everything. Everything except Emma's money, which Bart knew was stashed all over the trailer. He'd found over a thousand dollars just in the kitchen, mostly in old coffee cans at the back of the cupboard. He decided that getting his hands on all that money was better than a couple of days of free blow.

Bart's window of opportunity was closing rapidly. The storm would hit hard in a couple of hours and it was either now or never. If he took his findings to The Snatch Patch and holed up there, Emma would find him eventually, if she survived. He didn't like the idea of killing her; he'd never killed anyone before. Plus, people had seen him pick her up from the hospital. No, he had to just get far, far away and hope that neither Emma nor Tiny ever found him.

A report on the radio had said the storm would reach all the way through Florida, and the only safe places were out of state. That would be a long fucking drive, and he was getting shaky and nauseous, but he decided there was no other choice. He had to do it.

As Bart reached the northern edge of Key Largo, a patrol car filled the rearview mirror. The bar lights atop the officer's cruiser were flashing and then came the siren. Just a quick blast, but it was salt in Bart's wound. *Like I don't see you, asshole.* The speedometer read sixty-five just as he passed a forty-mile-an-hour speed limit sign. Once he'd put Islamorada behind him, the lobster crowd thinned out and he'd taken advantage of the semi-open road. Bart considered his options. *There's only one fucking road on these goddamned islands!* He figured that his chances of getting away weren't good, but thoughts of the dying body of Emma Hinkley in Islamorada made him consider making it run for it anyway.

"Sorry for speeding, Officer," Bart said in his best good-citizen voice. "Just trying to outrun the storm."

"Sir, are you aware that your tail lights are out?"

"Huh? They are?"

The officer turned sideways slightly to keep the pelting rain from blinding his eyes. "They are. Not only that, sir, it's too dangerous to be on the road. The

Sheriff's Office is strongly advising everyone to find shelter immediately. These conditions aren't conducive to safe driving."

Bart said he'd be sure to do that, and the officer was about to leave him in peace when he eyed a case of Bud Bart had parked in the front seat. "Have you been drinking, sir?"

"Nope," Bart said.

"So that open can of beer in the console isn't yours?"

Bart burped. "Negatory."

"What's your full name, sir?"

"Bruce Lee."

"License and registration," said the Florida Highway Patrolman.

Several months earlier, Bart's license had been revoked after his fourth DUI. It didn't really matter. He looked straight ahead, watching the torrents of rain come in waves over the pavement.

"Sorry, Officer, I lost my wallet last week and this car belongs to a friend. I don't know where she keeps the registration."

"Please stay inside the vehicle. I'll be right back." The soaking wet officer hustled to his car to run "Bruce" and the license plate through the computer.

While Bart considered any and all avenues of escape, a motorcycle slid into the parking lot of an outdated motel across the street. What had at one time probably been attractive cottages were now run-down shacks in desperate need of repair. The biker parked under an awning and stretched before stepping through the front door. No doubt seeking shelter from the storm. What a dumb ass to be out in a hurricane on a fucking bike.

Desperate times call for desperate measures. Bart opened the door to Emma's Honda, and darted across the highway. He'd not bothered to look before he leapt. A Budweiser tractor trailer heading north to outrun the storm clipped him just before he made it to the other side.

PATTYCAKES

Patty opened her eyes and didn't know where she was. The dim lighting masked her surroundings and her ears rang with the deafening sound of quiet. She pushed up from a thin, bare mattress and sat, listening to the muted stillness. Completely naked, she shivered in the damp chill. Patty felt the bite of hard steel clamped around both ankles. She fumbled in the dark, feeling with her hands and discovered that her feet were shackled to a heavy ring buried into the cement floor. Patty yanked at the metal constraints, sending a thunderous clatter to ricochet off the walls as the chains banged against the concrete.

What the hell was going on? She shivered and waited, frequently tugging at the steel bands around her ankles, hoping to find a way to release them. Eventually, her eyes adjusted to the darkness.

"Hello? Is anybody there?"

No one answered. Then Patty remembered the pills she took. She remembered feeling so good and happy for a few fleeting moments, and then nothing. That's where her memory went blank.

So where was she? Why was she shackled to the floor like a fucking war criminal? The darkness seemed to thicken. Patty let loose a desperate, primal scream. The resounding silence mocked her. She put her head in her hands and sobbed.

Patty's feelings of desperation quickly led to anger. "I've gotta get the fuck outta here," she whispered. In the dim light she could see the door was secured with a heavy padlock and chains similar to the ones that restrained her. There wasn't much to be seen beyond the bars of her cell except a few other cells on the other side of the room. They were empty.

"Hello?" She waited for a reply and then spoke more loudly. "Is anybody there?"

The only sound was the scurrying of a mouse. Maybe a rat. She tried not to think about it as she sat back down on the mattress and hugged her knees to her chest. She struggled hard to remember how she got there.

Her thoughts were interrupted by the sounds of footsteps and loud voices. Sam led a group of men toward her cell. She recognized one of them as the Sweat Hog she'd given a lap dance to and another as the bouncer at The Snatch Patch the day she'd gone for the interview. It felt like years ago, but Patty figured it had probably only been a day or two. They leered and laughed, fueled by booze and drugs. Patty shook with fear.

"Who's first, gentlemen?" Sam bellowed.

The Sweat Hog forced himself in front of the others.

"Nichols it is." Sam said. "Have at it, Jody. Enjoy the ride."

To the rest he said, "I'll leave you boys to your fun. Be sure to lock up when you're done." Then he smiled at Patty and disappeared.

Each of the six men took their turn raping Patty,

egged on by the others as they banged on the cell bars and laughed. She vomited acidic bile on the Sweat Hog as soon as he mounted her. He thanked her by splitting her lip before forcing her onto her stomach. He mashed her face into the stained mattress and rammed himself into her backside. She stopped fighting back when the pain took over. Mercifully, she was unconscious when the last man had his turn.

She woke while being rolled onto a bath towel that had been spread out on the dirty cement floor. After the mattress was flipped, she was hosed off with cold water that stung like hail stones. Patty wasn't capable of moving any part of her body. She had no strength left. Someone pulled her onto the mattress. The fabric was chilly and damp from being against the cement floor. Patty shook with cold.

"Drink this."

The voice was familiar. Patty forced one eye open. The other was swollen shut from a punch the bouncer had given her when she bit into his ear. "Get the fuck away from me!" Patty's shout was barely audible because her voice was spent from screaming.

"Patty, I'm here to help you." Carla put one arm around Patty's shoulders and brought the cup to her lips. "You need to listen to me if you want to survive."

Patty tried to push Carla's hand away, but her feeble attempt was pointless. "Fuck off."

"If you wanna live, you'll listen to me. If you don't, you won't make it through the next two days."

Patty began to cry. "What's happening to me?"

Carla put the bowl to Patty's lips. "Drink. Then we'll talk." Patty couldn't argue. Breathing and swallowing were monumental tasks. When the bowl was empty,

Carla lowered Patty to the mattress and then placed a hand on each of her knees. "I'm going to slather some medicine on you. It'll help the pain." Patty cringed as her legs were parted but was grateful for the soothing suave being applied to her damaged parts. She was almost asleep when Carla lifted the back of her head with one hand. "Take this," she said. "It's for pain too."

Patty felt two pills drop onto her tongue, which felt thick and dry. Carla put a cold metal cup to her cracked lips. She drank and swallowed. Pattycakes Farley was mostly unconscious when Carla stuck her inner arm with a syringe. When it had been emptied into Patty's vein, Carla covered the woman's ravaged body with a blanket and left, securing the cell door behind her.

Carla hadn't explained anything. And the nightmare had just begun.

Patty woke to the sound of men shouting, their speech urgent but slurred. Panic set in when Patty realized it wasn't a bad dream. The same group of men had returned, sounding even more wild and aggressive than before. Her sobs and pleas to be left alone brought on raucous laughter.

The bouncer went first and when he brutally forced her legs apart, she thought she may have dislocated her right hip. Her attempt to kick him in the nuts was met with an uppercut to the chin that knocked her out. It was a blessing, because the next one that climbed on top of her was ruthless. As he prepared to cum inside her, he bit through one of her nipples. When he climbed off her limp body, the tip of her breast hung crooked, bleeding profusely down her side and onto the stained mattress. She came to, about an hour later, as her sodomizer yanked her hair. One of the onlookers shouted something about police brutality and they all laughed. Patty's world consisted only of pain and the smell of sex. She prayed for death.

As before, Carla showed up after the men had tired of their game. Some of them had taken more than one turn. Carla set about the task of washing away the bodily fluids and blood and then applying suave to all of the parts that desperately needed it. Halfway through the sponge bath, Patty managed a weak whisper. "Please help me."

Carla sighed. "What the fuck do you think I'm doing?" She rolled Patty off the soiled mattress and flipped it. The blood and wetness from the previous raping session had dried and crusted. She rolled Patty on top again, oblivious to the woman's babbling and begging. "It'll be better soon." Patty felt a sting and a prick on the inside of her arm. She knew she was powerless.

HAMMOND

Hammond, Stella, and Matt were eating pita pockets stuffed with tuna fish for dinner. Hammond had insisted Matt have a real dinner, that bowl of sugary cereal from before just wasn't going to cut it.

They'd scoured Louis' office for an hour, and not finding his cell phone, had finally returned to the kitchen. Stella was visibly agitated while Matt had gone silent as the grave.

Trying to ignore the winds battering the canal-side cottage, Hammond took a huge bite of his sandwich and continued thinking out loud. "I've known Louis since I was Matt's age. He was my mentor when I first joined the force. Then he left, went to join the St. Pete PD for one reason or another, and I didn't see him again until he came back retired, and with a wife and kid in tow. The man had seen a lot, and more going on upstairs than he let on."

Stella took a small nibble of tuna fish and then put the pita pocket back on the plate, obviously not hungry enough to eat.

"You're telling us he was hiding this secret, other, better self from his family?" she asked incredulously. "He was a wreck, Hammond."

"Sure, the gin took its toll—but in my mind, Louis was brilliant."

Hammond knew Stella liked him, and was trying to be respectful, but he could see her barely holding back another angry retort. He figured he should hurry to the important stuff.

"So, when Louis came asking me for help a couple months ago, on that private case involving the teenage runaway—Gerry—I listened.

"Bit by bit, over the past couple months, Louis had been putting the pieces together.

But when I tried to bring some of Louis' leads to my lieutenant, namely that Louis suspected a man named Sam Schneider," Hammond pointed his thumb southwardly, "he owns that . . . gentleman's club, The Snatch Patch. Anyway, he suspected that Sam was part of a trafficking ring, Rice fired back almost immediately with documentation that he himself had surveilled Sam and inspected the place many times. According to Rice, the man and the place always came up clean.

"Look," Hammond paused to finish off the rest of his sandwich. "I just don't think it's fair that most people, including you, Stella, thought Louis was just a useless drunk, but that's the way he wanted it."

"Why would he want it that way?" Matt looked at the tuna salad he'd been sculpting listlessly with his fork instead of scooping into the pita and eating it.

Hammond wanted to get this answer right. It would mean a lot and make a difference in the kid's life. He recalled Louis trying to explain that the life of a private investigator was hard enough without getting the people you loved involved.

"*The less they know the better.* That's what Louis said to me about it. He wanted to keep you safe."

Hammond suddenly felt something tugging at his

sixth sense, and an image of Louis' cluttered office sprung to his mind. "Stella, when you went through the house Monday morning getting rid of all the booze, did you see Louis' cell phone then?"

Stella shrugged. "I think so." She was pensive for a moment. "Wait! I know I did because I remember thinking, 'that thing's about ten years past its prime, just like Louis.' It was like he was stuck in 2008, and then I realized he'd had that phone when I first met him, which was 2008! That ridiculous antique made me angry for whatever reason. I mean, I was already pissed that he'd nearly killed my child the night before, but that stupid old phone rubbed me the wrong way. I could picture him taking ten minutes to send a five-word text and it pissed me off."

Hammond waited until he was sure Stella was done. He marveled at the things that got under people's skin about their spouse, but knew better than to comment on it. "So where is the damn thing, then?"

"Well, it wasn't on him when he died," Stella said. "They would have told me, and I haven't seen it since."

Hammond looked further disturbed by this information.

"All I found was a clunky old walkie-talkie thing. Looked older than dirt."

Hammond's head tilted. "What sort of walkie-talkie thing? Can you show me?"

Stella disappeared and was back almost immediately. She handed something to Hammond.

"Whoa!" he grinned. "This is his old police radio. This was the kind they used when I joined the force. I didn't know he kept this." Hammond gave it a thorough once over. "I wonder if it works?"

Matt plopped down on the couch and Stella joined him, leaving her dinner mostly untouched.

Hammond turned the old relic on and the threesome was greeted with police chatter. He absentmindedly turned the volume down a bit and put it on the table next to him.

"Would Louis have had time to go to the store and purchase that gin while you were on the water?" Hammond said.

"Time isn't really the issue, Chris," said Stella. "You know we only have the one car, right?" She didn't wait for a reply. "And Matt had practice that morning. Since neither Louis nor I needed it, we told Matt he could have the car." She turned and faced her son. "Matt, you drove it to practice, right?"

Hammond noticed that Stella phrased her question a little archly.

"Yeah."

Stella's temper suddenly flared up at Matt in a way Chris had never seen.

"Jesus Christ, boy, stop lying!"

Both men stared wide-eyed at her.

"I ran into your coach. For Christ's sake, Matt, I know you weren't at practice Monday morning or at his house Monday night. So where the hell were you?"

Matt went white. This was one hell of an interrogation. Hammond was impressed.

"All right, all right. I'm sorry." He ran a hand through his hair. "I lied. I was with a friend."

"What friend?"

"Just one of the guys."

"Why?"

Matt shrugged. "I didn't feel like going to practice

and I hated being home with Dad. I just didn't feel like going to work, Mom. Don't you ever feel like that?"

Stella harrumphed. "And Monday evening?" she shouted. "What about then? Where the hell were you then?"

Matt threw his hands up in frustration. "Mom! Why can't you understand that I just didn't wanna be here after Dad, and the police, and . . ." Matt's voice grew soft and melancholy. "I just didn't wanna be here."

Stella softened. She was worried about her son. "Okay, I get it, but just be honest with me, okay? You can tell me anything."

Matt nodded without making eye contact.

Hammond stood and began to pace the cramped kitchen. "Let's go over everything. What do we know? Louis begins an investigation into a local human trafficking ring. He asks for the department's help, but Rice won't give it. Louis has a strong hunch about The Snatch Patch and continues to investigate, keeping me informed on the low, but never really showing me evidence I can take to my captain. Sunday evening, while I'm sleeping, someone breaks into my squad car and steals my gun, my cell, and my radio. The same evening, Louis and Matt have an accident, Louis gets a concussion, and goes to the hospital. He comes home and promises to stop drinking. The next morning, Stella dumps out all the booze in the house, or we assume she does, and then goes fishing for several hours. Matt wakes up and takes the car to a friend's place to get away from reality, and then sometime later Louis wakes up and somehow procures a bottle of—what kind of gin?"

"I don't remember," Stella said. "But it was the cheap stuff."

"Didn't Louis only drink Sapphire?"

"Exactly," said Stella as she rolled her eyes.

"And right now, that bottle is in evidence, and probably won't be tested until after this storm passes, and the tox reports on the body probably won't come back until next week."

"You got it," said Stella grimly. She'd obviously gone over the timeline with the investigators already.

"Louis dies on the dock sometime, probably around one or two in the afternoon?"

"They haven't figured out time of death yet," said Stella. "The whole case is on hold right now."

"So, let's assume two. Louis gets up at his usual late hour, and either unearths a very hidden bottle of gin, or someone leaves it for him. He has a couple drinks, and it's is enough to end his life."

Matt muffled a sob and quickly got up to go to the bathroom.

Hammond wondered if this was too much for the kid to hear so soon after his father's death. "Stella, should we table this discussion? Maybe until after Matt goes to bed? This has to be hard for him."

Stella nodded in agreement. "Fucking Louis put my son through enough. Let's not add to it. This can wait. We're not going anywhere."

Hammond watched Stella stare off into space with a vacant start for several minutes. When Matt returned, his eyes were red and his face stained with tears.

"Hey, Matt," Hammond said, "I'm sorry. I should have realized how difficult it would be for you to hear this stuff right now. Let's talk about something else."

"No!" Matt insisted. "I want to hear all of it. Everything. I'm fine."

"Honey…," Stella began.

"Mom! I'm fine." Matt looked at Hammond with steely eyes. "Keep talking."

Hammond paused for a few moments and then nodded. He stood and clapped his hands. "Okay! We're almost positive that Louis' cell phone is missing, right? What if the person who brought the gin came inside and took the phone!"

"Can we trace it?" Stella asked.

"Probably not," said Hammond. "It was really old. I mean, maybe some of the guys at the precinct could, but we couldn't do it online or anything."

Hammond started pacing again, focusing on the thing ticking in his brain. He wouldn't put it past Louis to have a cheap bottle of backup gin stashed somewhere even Stella couldn't find. Louis had grown up in the cottage and knew it better than anyone. And there was the issue of the missing evidence. Could it have been taken with the cell phone? Or did he have a secret hiding place for it all?

"Stella, is there a single place in this whole house that we could possibly have missed?"

"I don't think so," she answered wearily. "But it's getting late and I'm tired of this detective bullshit. Let's get to bed and look again tomorrow."

Hammond wasn't ready to let it go, but he agreed anyway. Mother and son looked exhausted. After a brief hug between them, Matt retired to his room, his face ashen. Stella stumbled to hers and as Hammond watched her, he thought she looked older than her years. His heart aching for them both, he flopped on the living room couch, hoping the clattering of the walls would soon stop, and that nothing would blow off the house while they were sleeping.

He dreamt of Louis sitting on the dock holding a tall drink, a bandage on his head, looking at the canal, wordlessly staring across the water at the other side. When Hammond tried to talk to him, he saw that out in the water was a small figure, circled by massive bull sharks that sometimes wandered into the neighborhood canals. He looked closer and saw that it was Patty, flailing her arms and calling to him for help. He decided, in dream logic, to shoot the sharks from where he stood. He reached for the gun in his holster, but it was missing. He looked down. It was in Louis' hands. Louis was pointing the pistol at himself.

"No!" screamed Hammond, and the dream vanished. He opened his eyes. He was sitting up in the dark living room, drenched with sweat. Outside the storm raged.

DAY FOUR

PATTYCAKES

"Get up!"

A kick to the back woke Patty from a dead sleep. Not again. She couldn't go through it again. She rolled over and looked through her good eye. She knew the guy. He'd already raped her a few times and did his best to out-do his buddies in the rough and nasty department. She knew the type. Always had something to prove.

"Glad to see you're still alive, but man, you sure smell dead. I thought Carla was supposed to be keeping your sorry ass clean. Gonna have to talk to Sam about that."

Patty didn't say anything. As long as the man was talking, he wasn't hurting her.

"I hear through the coconut telegraph that you and that imbecile Hammond are friends. I find that very interesting." The man thoughtlessly tapped the side of a radio hooked to his belt.

Patty's breath, already ragged, nearly stopped at the mention of Hammond.

He sauntered around the cell, hands on his hips. "You oughta be more careful. When you whore around on this island, word's gonna spread. Just like your legs." He laughed at his joke before continuing. As he turned, Patty saw a holstered gun on his hip. This asshole's a cop? Where's Hammond? What if he's hurt? She swallowed hard. What if he's dead?

"As I was saying, Tiny spotted you and that fat ass Hammond drooling all over each other at the Lorelei. Interesting."

Patty's tormentor stopped pacing and faced her square on. "Know what else is interesting? I'm fucking his old lady and now I've fucked the life outta his whore too. That'll show that fat bastard what a worthless piece of shit he is."

Patty sat up, her fear temporarily pushed aside to make room for anger. "Who the fuck do you think—"

She didn't get to finish because the man delivered a precise quick kick to her side, knocking the wind from her lungs.

"I don't like to be interrupted when I'm talking, so keep your fucking mouth shut." He began to saunter again, a slow pace back and forth in front of Patty. "But I'm the kind of guy who strives to be better each and every day. Fucking the two of you worthless broads just doesn't feel like enough." He pulled a knife from the waist band of his jeans. "So, I'm gonna carve you like a Thanksgiving bird and leave your sorry carcass for your boyfriend to find."

The man admired the knife and then grinned at Patty. "That oughta teach him to mind his own fucking business, don't you think?"

Something inside Patty finally snapped. It'd been a while since her last dosing and she could feel her body, despite its many injuries and weak condition, surge with life and rage. She'd been scrappy in her youth, getting into fist-fights with boys at school and with her older brothers.

Patty gathered every bit of strength remaining and kicked the side of his knee as hard as she could. She heard a snap. When he dropped to the ground, she kicked hard between his legs. But it was when his head hit the cement floor hard enough to knock him unconscious that she realized her terrible gamble had worked.

Tears threatened to come but Patty knew she wasn't out of danger. Pull yourself together and get the fuck outta here, a voice in her head commanded. She twisted her body across his to grab the radio and keys, terrified he might suddenly wake and grab her. She fumbled from adrenaline but got the shackles unlocked from her swollen and bruised ankles.

Patty tried each of the keys until the cell door opened. As she closed it behind her, she could hear the storm raging beyond the cinder block walls of the club. The tell-tale sounds of the hurricane had been much more muffled within the confines of her cell. She locked the unconscious man inside and made her way down the dimly lit hall. At the far end was an exit to a stairwell leading to the backdoor of the club. Patty staggered up the stairs in pure survival mode, into the hallway, and then pushed open the heavy door.

It was nearly yanked off its hinges by the raging hurricane.

She'd managed to free herself from the cell, but what good did it do when she couldn't leave the goddamn building? Patty's body shook hard, she dropped the radio. It bounced away from her, out the door, and into the rain. As she tried to shield her face from flying debris, the massive door slammed shut behind her. She scooped up the radio and turned back to the door. It was locked. She fumbled with the keys she'd taken from the man, but none of them worked.

Patty stood alone. Naked, beaten, and weak in the midst of a hurricane with no hope of finding help. She pressed against the building and thought about Hammond. She'd made it this far. She'd gotten out of that cell and had to keep trying.

Patty crept along the wet cinder block wall to the other side of the building where another door led to the dormitory hallway. Turning the corner, she was nearly struck by an airborne trash can. She ducked and yanked open the door, barely able to keep from screaming.

Exhausted and shaking, she slipped into her room and locked the door, but she knew that wouldn't be enough to keep her safe. Using what was left of the fading adrenaline, she shoved a heavy chest of drawers in front of the door and prayed for the storm to end. She needed to get out and find help. She needed to find Hammond and tell him about Sam and Carla and about finding his cell phone. But there would be no contacting anyone until the storm had passed. Patty burrowed under her covers and waited.

EMMA

Emma woke, groggy and confused, and wanting. Her first thought was that she needed a beer and some weed, to start, and then whatever else she could get her hands on. She didn't feel picky. But that thought didn't last long. Suddenly the trailer—her whole world—rocked hard like something was trying to push the old tin can off of its cement footing.

"Bart!" she hollered.

After shouting for Bart a second time, Emma heard a window break. Her bedroom door was closed, but the wind rushed underneath it into her room. The curtains billowed and the rolling papers on the bedside table became sad confetti. Emma hollered louder for Bart, as her fear of the storm mounted.

Had he fucking abandoned her? Where the hell was he? Did he leave her to die in a goddamned hurricane while he ran for safety?

She decided to crawl to the bathroom because she'd heard that the bathtub is one of the safest places to be in a hurricane, although she couldn't understand why. Emma tossed back the covers and gasped. Her body and bed were covered in her own waste. Emma fought back sour vomit. She flinched as another window shattered. The storm grew louder, making Emma's already pounding head an agony to endure. She

185

looked about her disheveled room and saw the trash can overflowing with dirty diapers.

That fucking bastard! How long had she been lying here in her own shit?

He'd left her here alone.

Bart had left her here to fucking die.

The noise from the hurricane was deafening, like a deadly locomotive aiming straight for her bed. Emma covered her ears with her hands to protect them from the racket, but it didn't help. She screamed as the only window in her bedroom blew out, allowing Hurricane Patty's fury to fill the tiny space.

DAY FIVE

EMMA

Emma woke sometime later to more heavy rain, except this time, she wasn't watching it from inside her trailer. She was right out in it. Pushing up on her elbows, Emma eyeballed what remained of her modest home scattered like ashes all around her. Soaking wet and muddy, she ducked further under the plastic kiddie pool that had gotten wedged between her and a portion of her bedroom wall. It kept some of the rain off her, not much, but some.

Devastation was everywhere. None of the surrounding trailers had been spared and blocking the road, about fifty feet away, a small fleet of flats boats lay scattered like forgotten LEGOs. As she stared at the out-of-place boats, blood trickled into one eye and blurred her vision. She wiped it away with the back of a dirty hand and felt her head. It was caked with sticky blood. Emma tried to take stock of the rest of her body but was impossible to tell if her already useless legs were injured or not.

Emma felt stuck in slow-motion. Thoughts came only with great difficulty. She needed some weed, a pill, anything.

"Bart," she moaned.

Emma woke again much later to find she wasn't

alone.

"Hey, partner," said a female voice.

Emma could only see a pair of chubby feet crammed into neon orange pumps dotted with hunks of mud. The heels were broken off.

"Her eyes are open. You want me to get a statement or something?"

"No, thanks, ma'am. Let me do my job. Why don't you get back in the squad car like I suggested. This hurricane business isn't over yet and it's not safe out here."

"Alright, hold your horses," came the response. "I wonder if Boardwalk Pizza is delivering yet? I'd kill for a meat lovers with extra cheese. And some garlic knots. And several beers."

Emma heard a car door shut just as a police officer bent down and smiled. He looked vaguely familiar. The crevices in his knee-length rain slicker funneled rivers of water directly at her. Emma leaned away from the cascade, but it was pointless. The relentless wind blew rain at her from every direction.

"Ms. Hinkley, are you okay? Is anything broken?"

Emma shook her head. "My head hurts, but I don't think anything's broken, but," she hesitated, "I can't feel my legs."

The officer nodded. "But you couldn't feel them before the hurricane, right?"

She looked at him quizzically. "How did you know that?" Then she remembered.

"I recognize you now." Emma's mouth was dry, making it difficult to speak. "I guess I never apologized for what happened," she said, looking him straight in the eye. "I was so high, I don't even remember the accident, but I remember seeing you at the hospital."

This officer was the same guy she hit last spring when she was out of her mind on meth. It was that accident that ruined her legs.

"How come you didn't press charges? I probably would have if I was you."

Lopez dropped to a squat, pulled the hood further down his forehead, and sighed. "I wanted to, at first. I really did. But then I saw you in the hospital and found out that you'd never walk again. I figured you'd been through enough without me adding to it." Lopez paused. "Besides, my wife told me she'd beat my ass if I did."

Somehow that made Emma smile.

Lopez grinned back at her and then stood. He keyed his mic and hollered into it, hoping to be heard over the howling wind. "Good news, Ms. Hinkley, an ambulance is on the way to get you to what's left of the hospital."

"Oh shit, I almost forgot. Somebody tried to kill me."

Lopez shook his head. "No ma'am, it wasn't a someone. It was a hurricane and yes, it tried to kill all of us, but you're nearly out of the woods now."

Emma shook her head. 'No! Listen to me. A man by the name of Bart Levine has been staying at my house for a couple days, helping me, running errands for me, and . . ." Her voice trailed off, "Getting me pills. He left me here when I was passed out."

Lopez kicked at a pile of rubble before tossing his arms in the air, causing his hood to slip off his head. "You gotta be shitting me! After everything you've been through, you started that shit again?" His clenched jaw and furrowed brow did a poor job of masking his mounting anger.

"Wait a minute, please." She held up one hand, open palm facing the officer. "Let me explain. It was Percoset, I have a prescription. This guy, Bart, he must have been overdosing me and leaving me in bed. I don't know how long he did it, but I woke up in my own shit! Do you get it? He drugged me and left me to die." Emma's chest heaved. "I bet that bastard stole my money too."

Lopez took out a damp notepad and pen from an inside pocket of his rain slicker. After yanking his hood back over his forehead, he turned his back to the wind and prepared to write. "Start at the beginning and don't leave anything out."

When the EMTs loaded Emma into the transport almost forty minutes later, Lopez pressed a wet business card into Emma's cupped hand. "I'll come see you in the hospital as soon as I can, but if you remember anything else, call me right away. If you see this Bart character, call 9-1-1. Take care of yourself, Emma."

NIKKI

Lopez watched the ambulance drive away, wondering just how many lives Emma Hinkley had.

"All right, Ms. Mangione," he said, getting into the driver's seat. "You're coming with me."

"Well I sure hope so! My roof is gone and what's left of the trailer is more like a swimming pool than a home. And by the way, how many times do I have to tell you to call me Nikki?" The woman playfully slapped his arm. "We're partners now. I mean, first I help you with Louis Callahan's murder, now with hurricane search and rescue." She checked her reflection in the mirror of the passenger side visor and gave her frizzy do a quick zhush. "I mean, I won't be surprised if the mayor gives me a key to the city when it's all said and done."

Lopez rolled his eyes. "Don't forget about that little crime you committed, Ms. Mangione. That's why you're coming with me. My captain wants to speak with you."

"Oh, your captain, eh? Is he married?"

Fifteen minutes later, Lopez motioned for Nikki to sit down. Captain Zyra sat at her desk piled with stacks of paper and gave Nikki a tired smile.

"Ms. Mangione," she began, "Officer Lopez tells me you have some information that might prove useful to an investigation."

Nikki had practiced for this moment most of her adult life. She'd always hoped to be the critical link in a big police story and now was her chance to shine. She handed Lopez her cell.

"Will you record this? They'll probably need it later for the news."

"That won't be necessary ma'am," interrupted the Captain. "Lopez tells me you committed a crime. Let's start there."

Nikki pouted momentarily while she weighed her options. There weren't many.

"Well, money's been real tight since my husband moved out. Can you believe he went back to Tennessee to live with his ex-wife? I still don't understand it, but anyway, like I said, money's been real tight. I guess I mentioned it to one of the bartenders I know and she said she might know of a way I could make a few hundred bucks real easy."

"What bartender? Where?"

Nikki stuttered. "Well, I don't want to get anyone in trouble. I mean, she was just helping me out."

Captain Zyra didn't have time to waste. "Look, Ms. Mangione, the only one in trouble right now is you. You confessed to a crime and we will prosecute to the fullest extent of the law unless you give your full cooperation. You have about fifteen seconds to tell me what you know before Officer Lopez arrests you."

"Oh shit! Okay, well in that case, her name is Carla and she works at The Snatch Patch. She knew I couldn't pay rent this month and told me all I had to do was take some things from a guy's trunk. That's all."

"What guy? What things? Where was the car?" asked the Captain.

Nikki frowned. Her moment in the sun wasn't playing out the way she'd hoped. "I don't know who he was, but he lives in Islamorada. She told me to go to his house after midnight on Sunday because he'd be asleep. She knew that his trunk would be open and told me take the gun, radio, and a cell phone."

"And then what?" the Captain asked.

Nikki shrugged. "So that's what's I did. I went there, took the stuff, and then went back to The Snatch Patch. Carla paid me five hundred bucks." Nikki put an index finger in the air. "Hey, just wait a cotton-pickin' minute. I get to keep the money, right?"

The impatient look on Captain Zyra's face encouraged Nikki to go on with her story.

"Anyways, as I saying, Carla kept the gun and the cell, but said I could have the radio, so its mine fair and square. I'm planning to sell it on eBay after the hurricane." She looked at Lopez. "As soon as a certain cop gives it back to me. Ever hear of finders keepers?"

Lopez interjected. "She used the radio to call for help when she found her neighbor, Ms. Hinkley, injured and unconscious."

Captain Zyra raised her eyebrows. "Hinkley? Is that who I think it is?"

Lopez nodded. "One and the same."

"Interesting." She returned her attention back to Nikki, who chewed on a broken nail. "Ms. Mangione, Officer Lopez is going to hand you off to another officer to get a written statement. Don't leave town. We're not done with you yet."

"But," began Nikki.

"Not another word. Like I said, don't leave town."

Lopez opened the door and gestured to Nikki.

"Ms. Mangione, please wait outside for me. I'll be with you in a minute."

Nikki shot the captain a nasty look and clomped into the hall. Lopez shut the door and spoke in a quiet whisper.

"Emma Hinkley said that some guy named Bart Levine tried to kill her. Said he's been living with her for a few days, feeding her pills and shit. Apparently, he drugged her and left her in bed long enough for her to use it as a toilet. She came to as the hurricane hit and he was gone. I put out an APB."

"Karma's a bitch, Lopez. Have dispatch send someone over to Hammond's and tell him to get in here. I need to talk to him."

After passing Nikki off to another officer, Lopez switched from the dispatch radio channel to another that he and Williamson used. Cell communications were still down. After a quick conversation about their families and damage to their houses, it was back to business.

"Remember Stella Callahan's friend that I interviewed after Louis' death? Well, she confessed to stealing Hammond's gun and cell phone from his trunk. Said that a bartender named Carla at The Snatch Patch paid her five hundred bucks to do it. Looks like Sam Schneider might be interested in Hammond for some reason."

Williamson was quiet.

"You copy?" asked Lopez.

"Loud and clear," Williamson replied.

"We should talk to him. I'm coming to pick you up. Be there in fifteen."

Lopez stopped at dispatch on the way out and passed on the Captain's message. He hustled to his car, relieved to see that the worst of the storm had passed. The winds had dropped significantly but the rain continued to pelt the cruiser. Lopez tossed his wet rain jacket into the back seat and headed to his partner's house confident that Hammond would be cleared in light of Nikki's confession.

The radio squawked. "Hello? Hello? Can anybody hear me?"

Lopez turned up the volume. That certainly wasn't dispatch talking.

"My name is Patty Farley and I need help!" a woman's voice squawked through the radio.

Lopez listened in disbelief as a vaguely familiar male voice responded.

"Patty? Where are you?"

Lopez double-checked the radio to be sure he was on the right channel. What the hell was going on?

"Hammond! Hammond is that you? You've gotta help me! Sam had me locked in a cell—" The woman was sobbing and babbling mostly incoherently. Lopez couldn't understand much, but he definitely understood when she said "rape" and "prisoner." He listened as Hammond and the woman had a brief exchange in which he made her promise to stay locked in her room.

"Don't let anyone in!" he urged. "I'll be there as soon as I can. Keep your door locked!"

Lopez keyed his mic. "629, Dispatch"

"Dispatch, go ahead," came the reply.

Lopez let dispatch know that he and Williamson were on their way to The Snatch Patch as backup for Hammond in his search for Patty. He requested additional officers be directed to the scene to help bring in Sam Schneider.

Hammond's squad car was already in the strip club's parking lot when Lopez and Williamson pulled in. The three men huddled briefly in the downpour.

"Here's what we know: Patty's locked in a bedroom in the barracks with one of our radios. Sam probably knows she's missing by now, but it's unlikely he knows we're onto him. We should have the advantage of surprising him."

Lopez nodded in agreement.

"First, we neutralize Sam, then we find Patty."

"Hold on," said Lopez. "Don't forget that we've got at least two suspects in there. Carla's more than just a bartender for Sam. He had her pay another woman to steal the stuff from your squad car. She and Sam both need to be immobilized." Lopez scratched his head. "Hey, if your radio was stolen, what were you using to respond to Patty's call for help?"

Hammond offered a sad smile. "I guess you could call it a gift from beyond the grave. Let's go."

Weapons drawn, the officers approached a side door to the club, but found it locked.

"I guess it's the front door then," said Williamson as he headed for the front of the building.

"So much for the element of surprise," Hammond sighed.

The men slipped in the front door and quickly made their way up the red-carpeted stairs. The club was dimly lit and empty except for a very large man standing behind the bar. He watched the officers hurry in, each scanning the room with their guns held out in front of them.

"Can I help you gentlemen?" he asked.

"Put your hands in the air," Hammond said, aiming

at the hulking man.

"Whatever you say," Tiny said. As he brought his hands up from behind the bar, he fired his gun and dropped Lopez to the floor.

Chaos ensued as bullets flew through the air. Hammond pulled a table over on its side and took cover behind it. He reloaded and then popped up and fired two shots in Tiny's direction before dropping back down. Bullets came from his right as a new shooter came into view. Hammond shouted for Lopez as he backed closer to a wall and pulled the table toward him to provide more protection. "Lopez! Can you hear me?"

Men shouted across the room as guns continued to fire. Hammond radioed for backup and then popped up to fire in the direction of the voices. As he emptied his gun at the shooters across the room, Lopez slid on his belly to join Hammond behind the table.

"The bastard buried one in my thigh, but I'm fine," Lopez said before Hammond could ask. Blood oozed from the officer's leg, but he'd suffered worse and lived through it.

"Get rid of them," Sam shouted. "All of them."

Lopez fired over the table, but his bad hand shook and every bullet missed its mark. Rice joined Sam and Tiny and the three of them focused their firepower on the partially protected duo.

"You fucking traitor!" Lopez shouted at the lieutenant. "You piece of shit!"

As Lopez reloaded his weapon, bullets tore away chucks of the table.

Hammond shouted at Williamson, "Cover us!" as he and Lopez deserted the scant protection provided by what remained of the cocktail table to find cover behind a wall. When the two had nearly turned the corner, Rice fired and hit Lopez in the back. The man dropped to the floor once more as Hammond reached safety. Lopez was unconscious as Hammond leaned out and fired once, hitting Rice square in the chest. The lieutenant slumped behind the bar and out of view.

"Put your gun down, Hammond." Williamson aimed his Glock at his colleague's forehead. "I won't tell you again."

"Shoot him, you stupid fuck!" shouted Sam.

Hammond's eyes were wide. "You're with Sam?" he asked. "You can't be, brother. You just can't."

"Toss me your gun or you'll be as just dead as Rice over there," Williamson said, tipping his head in the direction of the downed lieutenant. "Do it!"

Hammond tossed the gun at Williamson's feet and raised his hands over his head.

"Face down. Now!" Williamson demanded.

Hammond shook his head in disgust, but did as he was told. With his cheek against the dirty floor he looked at Lopez, wondering if the man would survive before wondering about his own chances. What about Patty? He came to save her and just look at the fucking mess he was in.

"Come on!" Sam shouted.

Hammond watched as Williamson bolted across the room with the weapons and disappeared through a door with Sam. It slammed behind them. He immediately radioed while checking Lopez for a pulse.

"Dispatch, 461," he said breathlessly.

"Dispatch, go ahead."

"Officer down. Suspects escaped on foot, possibly to vehicles. They are armed."

"Copy. Backup and ambulance en route."

Hammond hesitated before continuing. "Officer Williamson should be treated with extreme caution. He is armed, dangerous, and in collusion with the suspects."

Lopez was breathing but unconscious. Hammond knew he had to find Patty before Sam and Williamson did. He stood and ran for the door they'd escaped through, leaving Lopez alone on the floor.

PATTYCAKES

Patty hugged the covers to her chest as the sharp popping of gun shots rang out. They were close enough to be heard over the rain that continued to hammer the building. Where was Hammond? She'd been holding the radio against her chest ever since she came to her senses and tried using it. What an idiot! If only she'd tried right away, maybe she'd be out of danger by now. But she'd been stupid and just dropped it on a corner of the bed while she waited like a sitting duck. Then suddenly it hit her. Duh! Use the damn radio. Fortunately, Hammond had heard her and she knew he was on the way. Sadly, the radio had since gone dead. She was alone and out of communication again.

Where were the cops? They must be in the club. Probably why all the shooting. What if the bad guys had shot Hammond? What if she never got away?

The abrupt knocking on her door made her gasp.

"Patty?" More knocking. "It's Carla. Let me in!"

"Fuck off," Patty shouted, fumbling out of the cocoon of blankets and walking toward the door. "You're no better than Sam!"

"Patty, you don't understand," Carla pleaded. "Sam said he'd kill me if I didn't do what he said. I had no choice!"

"I don't believe you," Patty spat.

"It's true. Please let me in! He's looking for me and he's gonna kill me if he finds me. He'll kill us both!" Carla was crying. "Please, Patty, let me in. I've got nowhere else to go." Carla continued to cry and pound on the door, rattling the door knob. "I'm scared!"

Patty softened a bit. She shoved the dresser out of the way and hoped she was doing the right thing.

As she was about to unlock the door, it flung open, keys dangling from the outside lock.

Carla stood in the opening pointing a gun at Patty. "You stupid bitch," she sneered. "Did you really think I was dumb enough to let you live? You're the only fucking person who can tie me to Sam's real business. End of the line for you, Pattycake."

Patty flinched in anticipation of the bullets just as Hammond raced in behind Carla and knocked the gun from her hands. Within seconds, he had her cuffed on the floor. Carla cursed and berated the two while they embraced.

"Oh Darlin'," Hammond whispered in Patty's ear, "I'm so happy to see you."

Patty's cracked lip bled as she attempted a weak smile. "Believe me, Hoss, you never looked so good." She pressed herself against the man she somehow already loved and closed her eyes. She was going to survive this goddamn disaster after all. Hammond held her tighter as the sound of sirens filled the room.

Patty was barely conscious during her ambulance ride to the hospital. She heard medical talk happening all around her, but the only sound that mattered was the soft, gentle whisper of Hammond in her ear. "Hang on, Darlin'," he said. "You're gonna be just fine." And she believed it too.

DAY SIX

EMMA

Emma watched as the woman who'd arrived the night before stirred in her bed. The man who'd come in with her had looked worried, stirring jealousy in Emma's gut. No one was worrying about her. She'd just managed to get the hell out of the hospital in Miami and here she was, a few days later, in a different one. Her house was gone. Bart was gone, that good-for-nothing bastard. Still, she almost wished he'd walk through the door because he'd at least be able to pass her some sort of pill. She really needed something to take the edge off.

She pressed the nurse's call button for the tenth time that morning. The bitches were ignoring her. They knew she needed pain killers but wouldn't answer.

Her roommate rolled over and Emma saw the woman's battered face for the first time. Either a jealous husband or the hurricane, she figured.

"Hey, roomie. I'm Emma."

The woman reached for the bottled water on her bedside table. "They call me Pattycake," she croaked.

"Looks like the hurricane kicked your ass even harder than it kicked mine," Emma said.

The woman scoffed and then took a long drink. "It was no hurricane and no, I don't wanna talk about it." She recapped the water and turned her back to Emma.

"Friendly," Emma observed. She pressed the call

button again, this time holding it down for several seconds. Then she shouted. "Hello? Anyone out there? I need some pain killers!"

"Jesus," hissed her roommate.

A red-faced nurse stuck her head in the door. "What seems to be the emergency?"

"I'm in pain. I need something right now!" Emma said. "I've been calling you all morning."

"First of all, you aren't the only patient here. Secondly, the docs haven't prescribed you any pain killers, and thirdly, you're being released." The woman disappeared without another word.

"Well, who the fuck is gonna help with that?" she asked no one in particular. Who could she call to come get her and where was she going if she found someone?

The man she'd seen the previous night returned. Emma thought he looked tired.

"Hey there, Hoss," Pattycake said. "Bout time you got here. You gotta bust me outta this dump."

The man chuckled and then took both of her hands in his as he sat on the edge of the bed. "You're not going anywhere, Darlin'." He bent and kissed her forehead. "Doc says you're not well enough."

"What does he know? I'm perfectly fine, and I hate hospitals." Patty pushed a hair from her face. "Besides, I've told them everything I can remember. I just wanna go!"

"Me too," said Emma. "I can't believe I'm back in a goddamn hospital. I just got out a few days ago after being in Jackson Memorial for four months. I swear, I thought I was gonna lose my mind."

Hammond stood to introduce himself.

"Oh, please forgive me. My name's Chris

Hammond. What's yours?"

"Emma Hinkley," she said, glad for the company. Without being asked, she told Hammond all about her accident the previous spring and the subsequent lengthy hospital stay. "And then, after all these months, I meet the guy again. If it wasn't for the asshole who drugged me and tried to kill me, I probably never would have seen Officer Lopez again."

"Hold on," Hammond said, still standing. "What did you say?"

Emma repeated her story about Bart living with her for a few days to help out and then waking to realized she'd been drugged and left to rot and die in bed.

"What's this guy's name?" he asked.

"Bart. Bart Levine."

Hammond scribbled the name on a pad he took from his front pocket and then looked up. "And where'd you find this character?"

Emma looked away and bit her lip. "Some dude, people call him Tiny, found him for me." Emma could feel the man's eyes drilling holes right through her.

"Tiny?" Patty repeated. "Was he a huge guy? Like the size of an ox on steroids?"

Emma nodded, but avoided making eye contact with either of them. They had no right to interrogate her. She had no reason to feel guilty and she hated that she did.

"Hoss, that's the fat bastard that . . ." Patty began.

Hammond's hand gesture quieted Patty. "I know, Darlin'. I know who Tiny is." He turned to Emma again. "Have you told anyone else about these gentlemen?"

"Yeah, sorta. I told Officer Lopez about Bart after he found me buried in the rubble near my house. He's probably the reason I'm still alive." Emma absentmindedly touched her bandage. "He said he'd be here to visit, but I guess he forgot."

Hammond shook his head as he rejoined Patty on the edge of her bed. "No, he didn't forget. He's here. In ICU. Was shot yesterday. Don't know if he'll make it."

"What the fuck?" Emma whispered. "Who shot him? Why?"

"While responding to an incident at the local strip joint yesterday, Lopez was shot in the back by one of the bad guys."

"Oh my God," Emma said and then covered her mouth with one hand. "Is he okay?"

Hammond shrugged. "He's in ICU. Only time will tell."

"What happened to the guy who shot him?"

"He's dead," Hammond said.

Emma hugged herself and decided that when she was released, she'd find Lopez and wait for him to wake up. He had to make it. Besides, maybe she could steal one or two of the pills they were no doubt feeding him. They were probably keeping him so drugged that he wouldn't miss a dose here and there. Emma eavesdropped as Hammond and Patty spoke quietly on the other side of the small room.

"Darlin', I can't stay. Just wanted to make sure you're okay. I've got a lot to do."

Emma glanced at them sideways as Hammond held Patty's hands. "We're pretty sure we've ID'd the men who . . . well anyway . . . because of the details you were able to remember, we're pretty sure we know who we're looking for."

"You know who they are?" Patty asked.

Hammond nodded as he straightened her covers. "Most of them."

"I want to know their names," she said. "Tell me."

Hammond took a deep breath. "Well, you already know about my lieutenant, Rice. You also recognized Tiny." Patty nodded. "Then there's the coroner, Jody Nichols. We're not certain about the other two yet."

"And Sam?" she asked.

"He got away. So did Williamson and Tiny, but the entire county is looking for them."

Emma watched Patty's mouth tighten into a straight line. "Find them," she whispered. "Go find them and then get me outta here."

Hammond kissed Pattycake's forehead and was gone.

"So, what's Tiny to you, then?" Patty asked after a few moments of awkward silence.

Emma didn't like the way the woman seemed to glare out of the one eye that was opened. "He's nothing."

"So, a complete stranger found that peach of a man to help you out?"

Emma really needed a handful of pills just to deal with her roommate who obviously considered herself some sort of authority. "He wasn't a stranger."

"Yeah, I figured. So, what was he?"

Emma furrowed her brow and felt the stitches they'd given her tighten. "What's it to you? You some sort of cop or something?"

Patty pushed herself up in the bed and glared at Emma. "I'll tell you what it is to me. Your buddy Tiny and his group of drug-popping losers raped and beat me. For days. While keeping me locked in a cell and chained to the floor." Patty's chest heaved as her voice grew louder. "You feel me, honey? You see what it is to me now?"

Just then, a nurse pushed a wheelchair through the door. She up picked some papers from the seat and handed them to Emma along with a pen she had tucked behind her ear. "Just sign these, and you're free to go, Ms. Hinkley."

Satisfied with the paperwork, the nurse helped Emma into the chair and wheeled her out of the room. She avoided her roommate's angry glare, relieved to put some space between them. What happened to Patty wasn't her fault and the woman had no right to imply she was somehow responsible for it. Hell, it's not like the past few days had been any picnic for her! She'd been drugged and left to die in a heap of her own shit.

Emma almost pushed herself back to the room to remind Patty of that but was completely derailed by what she saw across the hall.

Emma closed her eyes and then opened them again.

He was still there.

She slowly rolled toward the open door. The man in the bed was awake, starring at the ceiling. She rolled close enough to be certain it was him. He'd been lying in a bed across the hall from her and she hadn't known. Briefly, she imagined how she might have snuck into his room in the night and suffocated him with a pillow or bashed in his head with a bed pan, but it didn't last. She knew she wasn't capable of that kind of violence.

"You fucking piece of shit," she hissed.

Bart Levine lifted his head and gazed at Emma with wide eyes. As he mumbled words she didn't understand,

Emma looked more closely at the bed-ridden man and then she grinned. Her smile turned to laughter and, eventually, to tears.

"I never believed in Karma," she whispered.

Emma absentmindedly wiped her cheeks with her fingertips as she stared. Her eyes were drawn to the middle of the bed, to the peculiarly empty space below his waist. Bart's legs were gone.

STELLA

Stella woke on the sofa to find the sun shining. From between boards attached to a living room window, she surveyed the damage to the yard and dock, finding she didn't really give a damn about any of it. She couldn't afford to stay in their house anyway, with Louis gone. She was going to have to sell, and after a hurricane, real estate prices aren't exactly on the rise. Where the hell would they go? And what about sending Matt to college? The bitterness and anger toward her dead husband returned.

As she started the coffee maker, the front door opened.

"Stella? It's Chris."

"Come on in." Stella rubbed her eyes and wondered how long it'd been since she'd had a decent night's sleep. She lit a cigarette as Hammond walked into the small kitchen.

"Got some news," he said. "But first, I'd kill for a cup of coffee."

Stella grabbed two mugs while Hammond busied himself peeking through gaps in the boarded-up windows and commented on the damage. She wasn't really listening. She was still thinking about where the hell she and Matt were going live when the bank took their house away. She wasn't a betting woman, but if she had been, she'd certainly wager they'd lose the house before someone actually bought the damn thing.

"Hey, Mom. Chris."

Matt had emerged from his bedroom. Stella first noticed the dark circles ringing her son's eyes and then his drawn mouth. He didn't look well.

"Hey there, Matt," Hammond said. "I came over because I need to talk with you and your mom. I know what happened."

Matt's face went white as he shuffled to the recliner and plopped down.

"So, your friend, Carla," he began, "is behind bars. They took her statement last night."

Matt's mouth dropped open. "Okay, look. I was gonna tell you today. Honest, I was."

Stella looked on with a sour feeling rising in her stomach.

Hammond rested his back against the fridge and crossed his arms over his chest. "Carla was working with Sam Schneider, the owner of the strip club. He's involved with trafficking kidnapped girls and she helps out by keeping them drugged and quiet until he can unload them."

Stella's eyes grew large as she looked incredulously at her baby. What kind of people was he hanging out with?

"No," Matt said, shaking his head. "That can't be true."

"Oh, it's true. And it gets worse. Carla and Sam had a friend of mine chained to the floor of a jail cell and allowed a bunch of thugs to beat and rape her over and over."

Chris turned and punched the lime green Frigidaire

then immediately apologized to Stella.

She had never seen Chris Hammond so enraged.

"I'll give you one guess as to who arranged to have my gun, phone, and radio stolen from my car." Hammond stood in front of Matt. "Come on, Matt. Take a guess!" The boy was silent. "Nothing? How about some more clues, then? Guess who organized the theft of your dad's cell phone from this house?" Hammond shouted. "And his death!"

"Chris!" It was Stella's turn to shout. "Don't you dare try to blame Matt for what this Carla woman did!" She spat the name like poison. "This is not Matt's fault!"

"The hell it's not!"

Then Hammond checked himself and said more softly. "You wanna tell her, Matt? Or should I?"

Stella froze.

"I'll tell you everything, Mom, but please just let me finish before you start yelling."

Stella didn't want to hear any more. She wanted to walk away and forget everything.

"So, I wasn't making any money being assistant coach and I knew you and Dad were never going to be able to afford college. I really want to go, Mom. I hate it here and I knew I had to do something."

Stella's face hardened.

"The thing is, I found a way to make money. Good money." He paused and took a deep breath. "I've saved enough to get through my first year already." Matt offered a lame smile that his mother didn't bother to return.

"Just what the hell did you do to get that money?" Stella clenched her fists, concentrating on the feel of her fingernails digging into her palms.

"Carla knew I needed help, so she found me some work." Matt looked at the floor and then spoke quietly. "Selling drugs."

Stella reached for the closest thing, which was a coffee mug, and threw it at the floor. It broke into several pieces, which the group ignored.

"Selling drugs?" she shouted. "You sell drugs?"

Matt held up his hands. "I know! I know, Mom," he said. "I get it."

"Oh, I don't think you do, Matt. You're still missing an important piece of the story," Hammond said. "Why don't you tell your Mom who you were really with when you told her you went to hang out with 'one of the guys'? You know, when you lied about going to practice on Monday?"

More lies? Stella really hated the world and everyone in it. She wished she'd never married or became a mother. Everyone always lets you down and, in the end, you've got nothing to show for years of hard work but heartache and loneliness.

"What's the big deal about where I was anyway?" Matt's color had returned. "I'm not the one who was always drunk or wasting money on booze! I earned my money and I'll take care of myself!"

"Answer the question," Stella said. "Where were you?"

"At a friend's," he hissed.

"What friend?"

"The one you don't like. Carla."

Stella looked livid. "Selling drugs?"

"Just hanging out. She's older. And she's cool. She doesn't treat me like a stupid kid. And like I said, she's helping me out."

"And what was so important that you had to be with her after your father's death instead of staying here and talking to the police?"

"Because, Mom, for this very reason!" Color returned to Matt's face and Hammond saw a resemblance to Stella as he furrowed his brow. "I didn't want to be yelled at by you when you found out that I was with her instead of at practice with coach when Dad . . ."

Matt's eyes started to go red and he looked away.

"And now I feel even worse because I told her all about Dad's concussion and that if he drank any alcohol it would probably kill him. She knew all of that!" Matt was crying. "What if she's the one who put the gin out there for him? What if it's all my fault that he's dead?"

An inconsolable Matt sobbed as he flopped on the sofa.

Stella immediately pulled her son into her arms. "Oh, Matty, don't say that. It's not your fault. You didn't mean to hurt anyone."

"Are you listening to yourself, Stella? Carla is behind all of this mess and Matt's the reason why!" Hammond's face was hard and his eyes were narrow slits.

"Shut the fuck up, dude!" Matt jumped to his feet. "Go play cop somewhere else!"

"Matthew Charles!" Stella yelled. "That's enough." She pointed at Hammond. "You're no better! Take a seat and shut the fuck up. I'm tired of the two of you."

The two men did as they were told and waited for further instructions from Stella, who suddenly felt fully capable of putting the mess to bed. She went back to the coffee maker and poured herself a cup. She took a quick gulp and walked toward the silent men.

"Clarify," she said, pointing at her son. "When you were at Carla's the morning your father died, you're certain you told her about his concussion? About how alcohol could kill him?"

Matt nodded. Stella took another gulp of hot, black coffee. It helped her think.

"Chris, your turn. Did Carla share that information with Sam? Is he the one behind Louis' death?"

Chris nodded.

Stella finished the coffee and went back to the pot for a refill.

"And where is this piece of shit Sam now?"

"We're looking for him," Hammond replied, with far less bravado than before.

"Mom," Matt said, "I . . . I didn't know. I swear . . ."

Stella waved his words away. She knew that, despite what else he was doing, Matt could never intentionally say or do anything that would get somebody killed. He just wasn't that sort of kid, but then again, she couldn't believe he'd been selling drugs. Maybe she didn't really know her son. Hell, she hadn't really known Louis either.

What the fuck had she been doing with her life?

"Here's the thing, guys," Stella sighed. "Arguing about who did what won't change that Louis was a drunk, nor will it pay the insurance on this house or pay for college. I don't know about you two, but I'm tired. I'm tired of all of this."

"Stella, Matt," Hammond said. "Please forgive me. I'm exhausted and very worried about my friend who was, well, anyway, I didn't come over here to shout at you. Or to point fingers. I'm sorry." Hammond offered his hand to Matt. "I never should have blamed you, Matt. I'm sorry. Friends?"

Matt nodded and the two exchanged a brief embrace. Stella's face never softened. Their show of affection did nothing to lighten her heart, which was still full of anger at Louis. All of this was his fault.

"I actually have good news," Hammond said. "You won't believe it either. I came over first to tell you that we know who tried to kill Louis and why, but I got sidetracked." He looked at Matt again. "Sorry, dude."

"You're good," Matt said. He went to the fridge for a Coke. As he passed his mom, he kissed her cheek and smiled.

"Smile all you want, boy, you're still neck-deep in shit's creek," Stella said. "So, what's this news, Hammond? You've been such a ray of sunshine this morning, that I can hardly wait."

Hammond smiled. "Please. Stella, have a seat." He gestured at the sofa and waited for her to refill her coffee before settling in, her legs tucked under her. Matt sat next to her, guzzling the soda.

"Okay, I'll make this brief. We've already talked about how Louis was on to a human trafficking ring. Turns out Sam was the kingpin and he realized that Louis was poking around. Getting pretty close, too, because when Carla shared with him the information about Louis' concussion and what alcohol would to do him, he sent a guy named Tiny over here with a bottle of booze." He stopped and looked at Matt who instantly looked guilty and sick again. "Not your fault, Matt. Let me finish."

Hammond grabbed a chair from the kitchen table and spun it around. He sat on it backwards with his arms crossed over the back. "Apparently, when Tiny got here to deliver the package, poor Louis was already dead in his chair on the dock with a bottle at his feet." He tapped the side of his head. "Which reminds me that we still don't know where Louis got that bottle, but you can stop worrying, Matt. Now that I think about it, I'm pretty positive it wasn't because of anything you told Carla."

Matt grinned at his mother who ignored his sudden good humor.

"Anyway, Tiny came in and searched the study, and stole Louis' cell phone. That of course contained texts between him and me about Louis' investigation as well as some evidence. Pictures mostly. That, of course, is the reason my things were stolen. Sam could destroy both of our cell phones and all of the evidence along with them. With Louis dead, no one really knew anything."

"None of this sounds like good news," Stella said, irritation dripping from every word.

"Hear me out," Hammond replied. "I'm just getting to the good stuff. Remember the girl I told you about, the one bar backing at the Lorelei, who'd runaway?"

Stella shrugged. Truth was, she didn't care anymore. That girl wasn't her problem. She had plenty of her own. Glancing at Matt, she briefly wondered if she needed to send him to rehab. Ha! As if she could afford it.

"Her mother offered Louis a handsome reward if he could find her. Luckily, before Sam could destroy our cell phones, my friend forwarded the entire conversation to her own. As a result of Louis' investigation, the girl has been found."

"Yay," Stella replied, monotone. Chris's ear-to-ear grin annoyed her. She wished he'd leave.

"Don't you get it?" Hammond asked. "The reward money! It's yours!"

Matt jumped up to high-five Hammond. "Dude! How much?"

Hammond knelt in front of Stella and spoke more quietly. "Stella, you're going to be paid enough money not only to send Matt to college, but to keep yourself quite comfortable for the next several years."

"What did you say?" she asked.

Hammond repeated his words while Matt raced around the small cottage, shouting and fist-bumping the air.

Stella knew it couldn't be that easy. "What's the catch?" There always is one.

"There is no catch. You're a pretty wealthy woman, Stella Callahan."

The roller coaster of emotions was too much. Stella cried, grateful for those who keep the faith despite terrible odds. Through tired, happy tears, she watched the men hug and high five, only to do it all over again. In that moment, Stella's heart hurt less than it had for years. Maybe she'd been too hard on Louis. After all, he reunited a mother and daughter, and in so doing, provided for her and Matt's future. A small measure of forgiveness made its way into her heart and, this time, she allowed it stay.

HAMMOND

Hammond had been home for less than ten minutes when Carrie walked in. He'd stopped in for a shower and change of clothes on his way to the hospital to check on Patty. His wife had been gone for four days. Not once had she called to make sure he'd survived the hurricane. Maybe she didn't care. Truth was, he hadn't even missed her and that made him think hard about their future.

Since almost kissing Pattycake Farley, he'd been debating whether or not staying married "just because" was the right thing to do. Should two people who don't love each other keep pretending, even though neither is happy? Just because of a promise made decades ago? Until about a week ago, Hammond's answer would have been a definitive "yes," but things had changed. That equation was no longer as cut and dry as it had been. Before Patty.

At some point, Hammond had accepted the idea of living the rest of his years in a loveless marriage, slighted and avoided by the very person who should love him the most, because that's what he'd promised to do. But what about Carrie's promises? Didn't she make them too? What about her vow to love and treasure? She'd stopped making good on that promise years ago. Why should he fight to keep alive what she no longer valued? Things suddenly came into very sharp focus.

"Carrie," he said, sliding his recently-returned cell into a front pocket, "it's time for a divorce. It's what you've wanted for a long time and I think you're right. Hire an attorney, send me the papers, and let's put an end to this act."

"Listen, if this is about Rice," she began, "he meant nothing to me. I don't even know why I did it. I guess I was just bored."

Hammond watched his wife plop down on the bed they hadn't made love in for a very long time. That Carrie had left him years ago and he'd been waiting around for her to return. The mention of his dead lieutenant was like a bucket a cold water to the face. Shocking and painful.

"What about Rice?" he said as calmly as possible. He didn't want her to know he was surprised.

"He meant nothing to me, Chris."

"You slept with him?" he asked, steadying himself by resting a hand on a dresser.

Carrie shrugged. "It was no big deal."

She didn't even sound sincere. In fact, Hammond realized that she sounded bored. She was confessing to an affair with a dirty, killer cop and she sounded bored.

"And did you ever talk with him about me?" Hammond was beginning to connect the dots.

"I mean, I guess, sometimes I vented. Isn't that what married people do?"

Hammond did his best to use his cop instincts. He needed information. Getting emotional and angry would shut her down and shut her up. He needed her to talk.

"Sure it is. Most people do, I suppose. So, what

sort of stuff did he help you with?"

Carrie seemed satisfied that her husband understood her decision to confide in someone else. He watched her confidence grow as she continued.

"Well, you know how irritated I got when I'd text you to pick up something on the way home from work and you'd never answer? Because you never saw my freaking texts? Because you always left your damn cell phone in the trunk." She snorted. "God, that pisses me off! Who the hell puts their cell in their trunk, anyway?"

Hammond shrugged and resisted the urge to punch a wall.

"And your endless fascination with that old fart, what's his name? The drunk, ex-cop who thought he was a detective?"

Carrie's laugh made his skin itch. She sounded ridiculous.

"What a joke!" she continued. "Instead of taking me out on the boat and showing me off or taking me shopping in Miami, you'd go eat a greasy, fattening breakfast with that loser. How do think that made me feel, Chris?"

There it was. Carrie was jealous of Louis, so she found someone to listen to her. And fuck her too, apparently. It blew Hammond's mind that the person would end up being his good-for-nothing lieutenant. His wife had given Rice—and therefore Sam—enough information to make he and Louis serious targets, which is why Tiny had been sent to end Louis' life.

But if that druggy bartender Carla was telling the truth and Louis was already dead when Tiny arrived, then who had left the bottle of cheap gin for his old friend to drink?

Carrie's chatter took on a whiny quality. He'd have to think about Louis later.

"Did you hear me, Chris?" she asked, filing her fake fingernails. "I'll take you back if you just try a little harder."

Hammond laughed. "You're fucking, crazy, you know that, Carrie?" He packed an extra set of clothes into the bag lying near the foot of the bed. On his way to the bathroom to grab his toothbrush and electric razor, he spoke over his shoulder. "File the papers. We're done. For good."

Hammond felt more positive about the future than he had in years. He knew he was doing the right thing. As he walked into Patty's hospital room, she broke into a big grin. Her bruises were still quite bad, but the cuts on her lips were mending. She looked beautiful.

"Hoss!" she said. "You look suspiciously happy. What've you been up to?"

He bent and kissed her on the mouth, careful not to hurt her. She grabbed him with both arms and pulled him to the bed, wrapping herself in his arms. She felt so warm and good. She felt like home.

"You sure look good, Darlin'," he whispered. "I've missed you."

Patty released him from her grip and rearranged the neckline of her hospital gown. "Did you hear the good news?"

Hammond loved to see her smile. Her whole face lit up. "Tell me."

"I'm going home today!"

He hugged her a second time. "That's the second-best news I've had all day."

Patty furrowed her brow. "Them's fightin' words,

Hoss. What could have been better news than that?"

Her immediate transition from happy to full-on assault made him laugh. He had planned to make her wait, but he couldn't bear to see her unhappy. Hammond cleared his throat and became serious.

"What is it?" Patty asked. "Tell me."

"I told Carrie that I want a divorce."

"You're shitting me," came Patty's reply.

"Nope. It's over. Do you remember when we met at the Lorelei and you told me that I said I was married but I never said I was happy?"

Patty nodded and Hammond took a deep breath.

"You were right, and I've been thinking about it ever since. I wasn't happy. At all. I was staying married because I thought it was the right thing to do." He smiled and pushed a red lock of hair behind Patty's ear. It popped right back out again. "But then I met you and I realized that I was stuck. A loveless marriage just isn't worth doing. For any reason. You showed me that."

A tear formed at the edge of Patty's eye and Hammond wiped it away. Another followed.

"I deserve to be happy. We both do."

Patty nodded in agreement.

"And I know who makes me happy. It's you, Pattycake Farley. I love you."

Patty's tears flooded her cheeks, but her smile never faded. Hammond held her hands as they took turns laughing and then crying. Hammond had never been so optimistic about life.

"Hey, guys," came a voice from the door. "Sorry to interrupt, but there's something I want to show you."

Hammond turned to see Patty's former roommate. She'd rolled her chair just over the threshold.

"Patty, can I borrow him for a minute?" she asked.

Patty nodded and grabbed a tissue from the bedside table. "He's all yours."

"Ms. Hinkley, is it?" Hammond stood and walked toward her.

She nodded. "Call me Emma. Do you have a second? Someone wants to talk to you."

Hammond winked over his shoulder at Patty and then followed Emma to a room across the hall. The man in the bed looked haggard and rough. He'd seen the type before. An existence ruled by drugs.

"This," Emma said, pointing both index fingers at the bed, "is Bart Levine."

Hammond raised an eyebrow inquisitively. "No kidding. The same one you told me about?"

"One and the same," Emma replied. "He wants to confess."

The man gestured to a chair next to him. "Take a load off," he said. "I don't bite."

"Or walk!" laughed Emma.

As Hammond's eyes adjusted to the dimly lit room, he saw that the bottom half of the bed was empty. The man didn't have legs. Funny, Emma hadn't mentioned that.

"So, you wanted to talk," he said.

"That's right. Name's Bart Levine."

"Chris Hammond. What can I do for you?"

Hammond listened and took notes as Bart described how he and Emma met after Tiny had sent him to collect her from Jackson Memorial Hospital. He spoke openly about the drinking, the drugs, and the sex. Now and then, Emma chimed in with a clarification, but mostly she let Bart talk. He didn't stop until he'd gotten everything out, including his plan to drug Emma, leave her unconscious, and steal all of her money.

"Karma sure did fuck me, though, didn't it?" he chucked softly. "I lost my legs. Just like Emma." His smile faded.

"Got what you deserve, if you ask me," Emma said matter-of-factly, without bitterness or accusation.

EPILOGUE

"Is that everything?" Stella asked.

Matt took one last look around the small bedroom and grinned. "Think so. Let's go, Mom."

Stella was weepy. She didn't want to be, damn it. There was no reason to cry. She turned and walked out of the room before Matt could see her tears. She didn't want him to worry about her or feel one shred of guilt for going away. He'd said as much the night before.

"Mom," he'd asked, "Are you gonna be okay when I'm gone?"

She'd smiled and said, "Of course I am, honey. I even quit the Cholesterol Hut, if that makes you feel any better."

"Finally! I hated seeing you work there."

"Well, I don't have to anymore," she'd said. "Thanks to Louis."

And she meant it. His investigation had brought enough reward money to make them comfortable. Stella was grateful to be able to send her son to a good school. He needed to get out of the Keys. Nothing good was waiting for him on that chain of booze-soaked islands. Going to college and meeting people his own age, with different life experiences, would be the best thing for him. Thanks to Louis, that's exactly what would happen.

"Well then, kid," she said over her shoulder, "let's

get you to college!"

Mother and son set off on a happy road trip to Virginia, during which they took turns driving. They talked a lot, mostly about the future, but a little about the past too.

"You know what, Mom? All the while I was hating Dad, there at the end, it's nice to know that he was secretly doing stuff to help someone. Maybe he knew it was too late to save himself, but he managed to save that girl from whatever it was they were gonna sell her into. That's pretty cool," he said, peeling a clementine and popping a large section into his mouth. "Just goes to show, you never really know a person."

Stella marveled at the wisdom of youth. What had taken her over fifty years to realize had come to her son in a matter of days. This boy was going to be just fine.

When Stella returned from getting Matt settled at George Mason University, she happily spent her days on the water. While picking up some produce and local honey at the farmer's market, she bumped into the partner of a former neighbor who was searching for someone to help with her eco-tour business. Three or four days a week, Stella took conservation-minded tourists on two-hour boat tours through the backcountry. She wove through the mangroves and flats, sharing her knowledge of the landscape and the wildlife that called it home. It sure beat schlepping stacks of pancakes and greasy sausage links for a pittance.

In order to give her customers a more pure and satisfying experience, Stella often cut the engine and let the craft drift close to the mangroves, giving them a better view of the iguanas sleeping on shaded branches and the small fish teeming just below the water's surface. As they floated down Snake Creek early one morning, they crept up behind a Bayliner. Those in the front of her boat began to snicker and point. As they got closer, Stella recognized Dave Grody. Although his back was to them, she recognized his Guy Harvey wardrobe and perfectly coiffed hair. Unaware that he was being watched, Grody was pissing over the gunwale of his boat.

"You're gonna need bigger and tastier bait than that little thing if you expect to catch anything," Stella hollered.

The tourists broke into raucous laughter as Dave quickly shoved his "bait" back inside his pressed khakis. Stella started her engine and waved at Grody as they passed. The man's face was bright red and he was scratching his undercarriage. Stella's belly laugh only made him scratch harder.

Bart's confession earned him a quick trip to prison, which he knew he deserved. He was prepared to do time for what he'd done to Emma. He'd serve out his years and then, who knows. He had lots of talent. He'd be fine. As long as he could avoid Tiny, he knew he'd be okay. Maybe move to LA and be the first legless male porn star. Maybe dealing from his wheelchair would be more profitable because the cops wouldn't suspect a cripple of pushing meth on school kids. His options were endless. Until his release, he'd eat, sleep, and stay alive.

A couple days later, the guy in a cell across the way was released and a new prisoner transferred in.

"Well, well, well," said a familiar voice. "What have

we here?"

It can't be. Please, God, no.

Bart looked up from his bunk. Directly across the narrow hallway stood Tiny, who grabbed his cell bars in both hands and rattled them as he shouted.

"You're a dead man! I know you're the reason I'm in this shit hole. I tried to help your sorry ass. Kept you in really good shit, gave you a sweet set-up with that cripple bitch, and this is how you thank me, cousin?" He slammed his open palm against the bars. The corridor reverberated the deafening sound.

Bart starred at the monstrous brute leering at him from the other row of cells. He must be dreaming. His legs had been taken and he would serve many years behind bars. Wasn't that sufficient punishment? Emma hadn't even died! He closed his eyes and put his head back down on the threadbare bunk.

Tiny continued to shout and threaten and Bart knew the words weren't empty ones. His cousin's rage was palpable and eventually instigated other hot-headed inmates to start arguments of their own. Two guards walked through, putting an end to the prisoners' brief excitement.

"Hey, guard!" Tiny hollered. "Better tell that girl scout over there to run fast out in the exercise yard 'cuz when I catch him, I'm gonna wring his fucking neck."

The guard stopped and laughed. "You got the wrong con there, Slim. That poor bastard can't run. He ain't got no legs." He and other guard laughed as they walked away.

Tiny's raucous laughter drowned out all else. "This is gonna be the best damn prison sentence of my life!"

A few months after living in a shelter, Emma found herself sharing a small, ground-level conch house with an outgoing roommate named Lyndsey Mae, a die-hard SCUBA instructor. The woman spent more time under water than above, but she filled their house with friends and laughter. Emma couldn't have asked for a better roommate, despite the fact that she left the windows and doors wide open with the A/C running.

After paying her half of the rent, Emma banked most of her pay from the Electric Co-op where she now worked as an administrative assistant. During the weeks and months after the hurricane, Emma visited Juan Lopez as often as the hospital staff would let her. Eventually, she joined the hospital volunteer group and sat by Lopez's side reading murder mysteries to him as he dozed. They forged a warm friendship and he put in a good word with a buddy at the co-op. Emma had been happily working there ever since.

For the first time in her adult life, Emma was clean. It continued to be a daily struggle, but she was managing. Work, her volunteer hours at the hospital, and life with Lyndsey Mae kept her busy. She occasionally thought of Bart and wondered what could have been between them under different circumstances. She considered visiting him in prison, but Lopez had talked her out of it. For now.

Lopez' recovery was a long one. A bullet to the back meant months of hospitalization, physical therapy, and mounting medical bills. Despite his years on the force, insurance only covered a meager portion.

"The wife and I are gonna have to work like dogs for the rest of our years just to put a dent in the fucking debt I'm racking up in this joint," Lopez said. "Honestly, brother, my wife would be better off if I'd bought the farm."

"Don't talk that shit, man," Hammond chastised. "That's not true and you know it. Besides, I've got some great news on that front."

Lopez raised his eyebrows but continued to scowl.

"Stella Callahan called me this morning," Hammond said with a huge smile.

"And?"

"And," Hammond said, "she and Matt want to help you. Financially."

Lopez shook his head. "No way. I'm not taking her money. I know she got some reward money, but she needs that. Her son needs it for school and she needs it to survive. Thanks, but no thanks."

Lopez crossed his arms over his chest and continued to scowl.

Hammond chuckled. "Who said anything about reward money? You may not have heard, but young Matt was recruited by Carla to sell drugs and apparently he did quite well. In Stella's mind, it's dirty money and she won't let Matt keep it. They're donating it to you to help with your medical bills."

The scowl on Lopez's face softened. "Really? I mean, is she sure they can afford it?"

"Dude, she said that if you won't take it, they'll find someone else. She is adamant that neither she nor Matt will profit from drug money."

Lopez grinned for the first time in days. "Well, shit! Sign me up." He waited a moment before asking in a hushed whisper, "How much dough are we talking about?"

Hammond leaned in and whispered back. "Forty-two thousand!"

The men high-fived and celebrated before things turned serious once again.

"I still can't believe this is happening to me, you know?" Lopez said. "And to be shot by a cop! My own partner! "It soured Lopez's stomach to know that the man he'd trusted his life with had been working for Sam.

"Any leads, yet?" Lopez asked. "Anything at all?"

Hammond shook his head. "Not really. Williamson and Sam seem to have vanished, but they'll trip up and we'll find them. We will."

Lopez sighed. "At least Carla and Tiny are locked up. Hopefully that creepy fucker Jody Nichols is put away for life. You know, it makes sense now why Williamson always called that fat fuck to so many crime scenes. I could never understand why he liked Nichols so much."

Hammond put his cell down. He'd been trying to text Patty, but he still hadn't mastered the art. "I never would have guessed that Nichols was on the take from Sam Schneider. Just imagine how many tox reports he falsified to cover up Sam's dirty work."

"Yeah, it's fucking criminal. Is the fat man talking?" Lopez asked.

Hammond shrugged. "Not really. He's trying to work a deal with the district attorney and I'm worried that he's just slimy enough to make it work."

"Who? Nichols or the DA?"

"That's a toss-up," Hammond laughed. "They're both corrupt bastards. Let's change the subject."

Lopez clapped his hands together loudly. "With pleasure. Let me guess? You and Patty gettin' hitched?"

Hammond grinned. "Not yet, but soon, I hope. This news is almost as good."

"Lay it on me, brother. You make lieutenant?"

Hammond rolled his eyes. "Hardly."

"Well, what is it then?"

"We're gonna be partners."

"No shit." Lopez smiled. "Hope you're better than my last one."

Three months later, Hammond and Patty sat at a swim-up bar in an all-inclusive resort in Mexico. The brilliant sun beat down on the white tourist flesh below, making it a banner day for bar sales.

"So, Mrs. Hammond," he said, kissing the tip of her nose. "What next? Snorkeling? Jet skiing? Gambling?"

Patty leaned back and closed her eyes. "Decisions, decisions."

"Well, Darlin'? Answer the question."

"Okay, Hoss," she replied. "Don't get pushy."

The bartender put two frozen, fruity concoctions down in front of the couple.

"I think I'd like to down this cocktail, take a second one back to the room, and perform some wifely duties on my handsome husband."

Hammond blushed. "Patty! Shhh."

She laughed loudly. "You're so cute, Hoss. Believe me, no one cares what we're talking about."

He shushed her a second time by kissing her mouth. "Some things are meant to be private, Darlin', and that's one of them."

Patty hoped she sounded believable. She really wanted to be interested in a good old-fashioned romp in the hay, but the very idea sickened her. She'd been faking interest since the very first time when she'd insisted that she was ready.

But Patty had convinced him that she had healed, physically and mentally, while hoping that it would get easier. It didn't. Whenever Hammond touched her below the waist, she had to suppress a scream. She was terrified it would always be like that. No matter how much she loved him, she dreaded having any kind of intimate physical contact.

Suddenly Hammond said, "There's no rush, Darlin'," he'd said. "We have our whole lives ahead of us."

Patty looked away, afraid that Hammond was somehow able to tell what she was thinking. She didn't want him to know how fucked up she really felt inside. It would get better. It had to. Until then, she'd have to keep it hidden. Fake it until you make it.

Her eyes settled on a young couple kissing in the pool. Their public display of groping and making out made Patty's stomach sour.

"Looks like you need some A/C," Hammond observed. "You're really flushed. You feelin' okay?"

"Listen up, Hoss," Patty said, ignoring his question. "I'm going to make a pit stop while you nurse that drink. When I return, I expect you to be ready for duty." She winked. "You got me?"

Hammond returned the wink and blushed again. "I got you, Darlin'. Hurry back."

Patty floated lazily to the pool's ladder, stalling for time. Maybe when they got back to the room, she'd pretend to fall asleep or she'd lie about getting her period, because she knew her shy husband would never question that. Patty didn't like being dishonest with Hammond, but she couldn't tell him the truth. She couldn't admit that the very thought of intimacy made her nauseous. Whenever they made love, Hammond's gentle, loving face transformed into that of a leering Rice or violent Tiny. What Hammond interpreted as sounds of ecstasy were actually ones of expertly disguised terror.

He deserved better than that. But she didn't know how to tell him what was really going on.

Patty fought back sour vomit as violent memories of the basement prison came flooding back. She was powerless to stop them and the guilt that always followed. "If I hadn't taken those fucking drugs. If I hadn't trusted Carla. If I'd listened to my gut. Or to Hammond's warning. It's my own fault those bastards got me because all I ever think about is getting drunk and getting laid. Now look at me. I'll never be able to be a real wife."

The endless cycle of terror and self-blame was crippling. It was so difficult to concentrate.

Where was the damn bathroom?

After having finished his drink, Hammond waited another ten minutes before going to look for his wife. They'd agreed to leave their cell phones turned off and in their suitcases for the duration of the honeymoon—a decision he thoroughly regretted an hour later when he still hadn't found her. After searching all of the logical places she might be, Hammond spoke with a security guard who was dressed as if he operated a theme park boat ride. Despite his questionable appearance, the man understood police work. Within moments, a subtle, but thorough, investigation of the grounds was underway. When that proved fruitless, the local authorities were contacted.

"Mr. Hammond," the guard explained, "I've spoken with the comandante of our precinct's Policia Estatal and provided him with a detailed description of your wife. He assures me that his men will be looking for her. They'll contact me directly with any information."

"That's great, but there's more to this than meets the eye. A few months back, my wife was the victim of a serious crime organized by the leader of a human trafficking ring back in the states. There's a BOLO issued for the men known to have been involved and that information also needs to be shared with your, what did you call him? Comandante?"

"Yes, comandante is correct. Forgive me, but what is BOLO?"

Hammond sighed. "Police jargon is so inconsistent. It's an acronym for Be On The Lookout. We used to call it an All Points Bulletin. What does the local department call it?"

The guard shrugged. "I don't think we have that, but you'll have to ask Williamson."

Hammond choked on the bottled water he was chugging. He wiped his mouth with the back of his hand and asked, "What did you say his name is?"

"Williamson. He's the comandante."

A cold sweat came over Hammond. "That doesn't sound like a Mexican name. Any chance you know this Williamson's first name?"

The guard dug through some paperwork on his desk. "Aha! Yes. His name is Tom."

"Did you know there is a BOLO out in the U.S.

for a Thomas Williamson, formerly of my very own department?"

"I don't ask questions. I'm sure you know that bribes and corruption are rampant among our policia. It's a problem that the government can't figure out how to solve or doesn't care to. Either way, I do my job, mind my own business, and go home to my family each night."

This couldn't be happening. Hammond wanted to ignore his gut, but the damn thing was usually spot on.

Patty was nowhere to be found and that fucking traitor Williamson happened to be the local police chief. Coincidence? Probably not. As Hammond tried to push away the worst of his fears, the guard's phone rang. The man spoke in Spanish, becoming louder and more animated as the seconds ticked by. When the guard tucked the cell against his ear with his shoulder and began banging away at his computer's keyboard, Hammond sat in a metal folding chair against the wall and began to make a mental list of people to call and places to search.

"Mierda!" said the guard, slamming his cell onto the desk. "Better start making plans to evacuate. There's a helluva storm headed this way."

Hammond didn't respond. His brain was on overload.

"Did you hear me? The Servicio Meteorológico Nacional just announced that a Category 4 hurricane is coming and the models show it making landfall about fifteen miles north in Puerto Morelos."

Hammond's mouth dropped open. "You gotta be shittin' me."

The guard shook his head. "Nope. It'll be here in less than three days." He stood and motioned for Hammond to step out of his office. "We're starting a mandatory evacuation plan. I've gotta go meet with the resort staff to get the ball rolling. I'd run for the airport if I was you, man. Get ahead of the crowds. The last place you wanna get stranded is Cancun airport."

Hammond stood and shoved his hands into the pockets of his swim trunks. "I'm not going anywhere until I find my wife. Now tell me, where can I find Tom Williamson?"

"I'll give you a lift," said a voice behind him.

Hammond spun on his heel to find Jody Nichols wearing a police badge and an ear-to-ear grin.

TO BE CONTINUED . . .

Acknowledgments

First and foremost, a huge thanks to Cresencio. Your unending belief that I'm able to knock everything for six gives me childlike energy to keep trying to live up to your expectations. You sure do make things more exciting.

Buckets of heartfelt gratitude to my publisher and editor, Nina Alvarez. You are a gifted visionary and a patient soul. Without your encouragement and probing questions, this book never would have happened. I treasured our collaboration and wish you a lifetime of heady autumn scents and toothy pumpkins.

A big thank you to my friend and former boss, Marc Halvorson, a retired police officer of more than thirty years. Your willingness to let me tap into your expertise in law enforcement and criminal behavior helped keep me on my toes. I hope you'll forgive the occasional artistic license I took with procedural protocols.

To Chris Mattson, a dedicated and highly respected investigator for the Florida Fish and Wildlife Commission, thanks for making time to give this novel a gut check. Your insight is very important and your thoughtful observations will continue to benefit readers . . . in a future novel.

Thanks to Carolyn Birrittella, who stepped in during the early days, when the waters were pretty muddy. Your observations and suggestions helped shape this book.

To my best friend of forty-seven years, Leslie Kofron. You've always been a big part of my story telling and you're a big reason why I'm still trying to tell them. How will we ever surpass Johnny Tremain?

To my children and those I consider my children, thanks for letting me think I'm still cool.

ABOUT THE AUTHOR

Formerly of Islamorada, FL, Patti Lavell now lives in the Finger Lakes Region of the Empire State. She is the author of the memoir *Confessions of a Catholic School Dropout* (2012), the novel *Fat Chance* (2013), and has been a contributing writer for *Florida Keys Free Press* and Keywesting.com. Lavell was the coordinator of a police academy in the Florida Keys, and currently serves as the Chief Financial Officer of a trucking company in New York.